ST. MARTIN'S

MINOTAUR

MYSTERIES

DEATH BY RHUBARB

Lou Jane Temple

St. Martin's Paperbacks

DEATH BY RHUBARB

Copyright © 1996 by Lou Jane Temple.
Excerpt from *Revenge of the Barbeque Queens* copyright © 1996 by Lou Jane Temple.

ISBN: 0-312-95891-9

Printed in the United States of America

St. Martin's Paperbacks edition/August 1996

10 9 8 7 6 5

Chapter 1

Heaven Lee sighed and wiped the sweat off her brow. It was the beginning of the evening but she was hot and out of sorts already. Early May had brought a heat wave to Kansas City. The kitchen was steaming. An exhaust hood over one stove had broken today, the dishwashing machine had gone berserk, spraying hot, soapy water everywhere and a bartender had called from jail wanting bail money. In other words, a typical Monday in the life of any restaurant. Unfortunately, all these crises were hers to solve. This was Cafe Heaven, her very own problem child.

Heaven peered out the small pass-through window where later she would push plates of risotto and lamb shanks and spicy hacked chicken to harried waiters. Monday night was busy at Cafe Heaven mainly because it was the night of the open mike. Poets, actors and musicians tried out their latest scene or song on Monday nights. Their friends rambled in to cheer or jeer, but that was three hours from now. As Heaven squinted into the dim dining room, she saw only four tables occupied.

Table One, a six-top near the window was filled with darling blue-haired ladies who lived in the neighborhood. They liked to eat early before, as they put it, "all the crazies came out." Tonight they were sharing three Blue Heaven salads, and a double macaroni and cheese.

Blue Heaven Salad

1 head butter lettuce, Boston bib
1/2 cup crumbled blue cheese
1/2 cup pecan halves fried lightly in olive oil
1/2 cup blueberries

Wash, drain and break apart the lettuce. Be sure to use the tiny "butter" colored leaves in the middle. Top with remaining ingredients and serve with raspberry dressing.

Raspberry Dressing

1/2 cup raspberries, fresh or frozen whole
1/2 cup raspberry vinegar
1/2 cup honey
1 cup olive oil

Place berries, vinegar and honey in the food processor. Turn on and slowly add olive oil. The dressing will be slightly thick.

Table Seven, a romantic deuce near the wall, had been the ongoing rendezvous spot for a married surgeon from the nearby Medical Center. The newest member of his surgery team, a nurse with red hair and freckles was his current prey. They smooched over martinis before the doc went home to his wife and big house in Leawood, Kansas.

Heaven liked redheads, and she felt a pang of sisterly concern for this pretty young thing. Even though technically she hadn't been born one, Heaven had adopted red hair as her own so long ago she was almost surprised when her roots started to show.

Table Nineteen housed four artists from Hallmark, the giant greeting card company. They were sharing a bottle of Brown Brothers Family Reserve Cabernet Sauvignon from Australia and some duck burritos, another house specialty. Hallmark artists liked to take meetings at Cafe Heaven because of the butcher paper on top of the tablecloths and the markers Heaven provided.

Heaven didn't like the crayons that most bistros supplied for tabletop art. The markers made much cleaner lines. They also cost a lot more, another reason she was always in the hole.

Table Twenty-four was hard to see from the kitchen but as she craned her neck to the left, a familiar face came into focus. It was Sandy Martin, her first ex-husband. He was with a woman Heaven had never seen before, a striking, dark, exotic-looking woman. The couple seemed very cozy, whoever she was. They were sharing a plate of risotto and a lamb shank and sitting close. The woman was feeding Sandy Martin risotto, and he, at least, had the sense to be blushing.

Bastard! Heaven thought. He just loves to show them off to me. As if I care after all these years. She'd deal with them later.

At the bar, a figure dressed all in camouflage was moodily nursing a scotch on the rocks. It was Jumpin' Jack, a neighborhood character still reliving his own private Vietnam nightmare, a condition made worse by the fact that Jack had never been to Vietnam. Heaven was moved by something as she gazed at Jack's familiar back, was it empathy, guilt, a longing for the way things used to be? In the early seventies Jack had been a gifted painter, the darling student of the Kansas City Art Institute. Heaven and he had known each other then. Either the drugs or the turpentine fumes or both had changed Jack. Reality left and paranoia came to visit. And stayed.

Three stools down a well-dressed couple was drinking champagne and whispering to the bartender.

"Sam, come here!" Heaven called a waiter to the window. Sam was the son of a friend of hers and was just like a son to her. He had grown from a gangly boy to a handsome young man right in the restaurant. He had just turned twenty-one, was topping out at six feet two with blond hair and blue eyes to die for. All the girls had crushes on him. A lot of the men did too.

"Sam, slip up beside Tony and tell him that if he's making a drug deal with those scumbags I'll throw him back to the cops I just rescued him from. Those two are bad news. They haven't seen daylight for months. They stay up all night and sleep all day, just like fucking vampires.

"But, Sam, be cool. Don't let them hear you. And tell him I'm not buying their glasses of Vueve Clicquot just so he can get a free line of cocaine later."

"Okay, eagle eyes." Sam grinned and headed toward the bar.

"Hey, Katy, come and say hello." It was Sandy, holding up his wineglass in a mocking salute and waving at her as she peeked out the pass-through.

Heaven's real name was Katherine O'Malley Martin McGuinne Wolff Steinberg Kelley. She had taken Heaven Lee as her stage name during a brief stint as a stripper in the early seventies, and the name had somehow stuck. Just like the red hair. Sandy liked to remind her he knew her when her name was Katy and her hair was mousy brown. What a guy.

As Heaven steeled herself for meeting the new girlfriend, a flurry of activity bought her a little time. Joe Long and Chris Snyder, waiters at Cafe Heaven, artists and actors, and the two responsible for putting together the Monday night shows had just arrived.

Chris was decked out as Barbara Bush while Joe had on an early presidential years Hillary Clinton outfit, complete with blond pageboy wig and headband. They were going to do their piece on the "Peaceful Transference of Power" tonight. It was dated, but it was a crowd favorite.

Hot on their heels was a group of four women with determined looks on their faces and baskets of clear plastic-wrapped fudge squares in their hands. They were the 39th Street League of Decency Fudge Patrol; moral guardians who normally held vigils down the street in front of the nude dancing juice bar, serving potential customers fudge to stave off their other hungers.

Heaven could only assume that a flyer for tonight's show had fallen into the wrong hands, and the photo of the boys dressed as girls had given the League ladies a new project.

Last but not least, in marched Jason Kelley, Heaven's most recent ex-husband. All of a sudden, the restaurant seemed very small. Heaven headed for the back alley to smoke.

Chapter 2

Angel Rodriquez peered through the blinds of his darkened second-story office down at Thirty-ninth Street.

A main, midtown, east-west artery, Thirty-ninth Street had suffered the victories and defeats of Kansas City in general. Like retired great boxer Muhammad Ali, Thirty-ninth Street showed that it had taken some punches, sometimes seemed confused, but still had its dignity intact.

Angel looked across the street at the string of businesses that revealed the mix of seedy trendiness that was midtown Kansas City. On one corner a dry cleaner had survived the ups and downs of the street for twenty years. Next to it, a vintage clothing store had just opened. Then came a biker bar, a leftover from the early 1980s when Thirty-ninth Street was neglected and overlooked by the city fathers, left to sink or rise to its own level. Nestled next to the biker bar was a hip fifties collectables shop; next to it a Laundromat, then a shop dedicated to selling cat stuff, things for and about cats, and things for cat lovers like cat earrings and socks. The strip was crowned by Cafe Heaven on the corner.

"You are next, mamacita," Angel murmured under his breath, gazing at the cafe.

Angel Rodriquez was a product of Thirty-ninth Street just as surely as the cleaners and the cat store were. This was his neighborhood, the place he called home. He grew up around the corner with his grandparents on Bell Street.

Back in the 1940s, before Angel was born, his grandfather, Paul Rodriquez, had made a good living for his family working as a waiter at the Hotel Muehlebach downtown. He bought their rambling two-story house from the Irishman next door, raised a vegetable garden and three sons. Paul and his wife scrimped to send their kids to the Catholic school down the street, along with the Irish and Croatian families who scrimped for the same reason.

When Angel's father, Ernesto, was killed in a car accident in 1955, Angel was just two. So Paul Rodriquez and Yvonne asked the young widow, Carla, their daughter-in-law, and her son to move in with them. When Angel's mother remarried and moved to Wichita, Kansas, Angel stayed right there on Bell Street in his father's childhood room.

In fact, he still slept there. The house was all his now. His grandparents died in 1980, within two weeks of each other. His two uncles had let Angel buy their shares of the house. They knew how much it meant to him.

Through the high school years and after, Angel worked as a gas station attendant, apartment fix-it man, short-order cook, bar manager for a lesbian club and hotel banquet captain, all on or around Thirty-ninth Street.

He had paid his dues, he knew the street and he didn't have a criminal record. It had all led to his most recent incarnation as slumlord or real estate tycoon, depending on your point of view.

Angel had been quietly buying up property in the neighborhood for five years now, a dilapidated store-front here, a one-story bungalow there. He completely controlled one square block on the north side of the street. He was chipping away at the south side.

Of course, Angel had a little help.

There were quite a few breaks for minority real estate buyers, city breaks on bringing things up to code, state tax abatements, federal assistance with mort-gages. It was a dandy little package of discounts if you knew how to put them all together. Then there were Angel's partners, men who would rather not have their names on a registry deed or a banknote. Men who were glad to help find the right bank of-ficers, the perfect federal loophole to help a nice His-panic businessman buy a little property. They would even put up some of their own money if they had to. But it was more fun getting free money from the chumps at City Hall and Jefferson City. That's where Angel came in.

At forty, Angel was a striking man, squarely built, black hair graying at the temples, dark eyes that flashed with laughter but were filled with sadness. He had recently taken to wearing expensive Italian suits. All in all, he had a persona that made him irresistible to women and had led to his wife leaving with the kids four years ago. But Angel didn't have much time for women right now, he was on the merry-go-round, pursuing the brass ring.

He kept staring out at this, his street of dreams, waiting in the dark to collect his thoughts for the meeting to come.

Sometimes Angel's associates got impatient. Sometimes they acted as though Angel weren't moving fast enough, as though they had a timetable they weren't sharing with him. Tonight they would pick Angel up for a little ride, a little talk about further acquisitions. Angel watched in silence at the window for the big Lincoln to pull up. His partners didn't like waiting.

Chapter 3

When Heaven stepped back in the kitchen she faced five new food orders and two ex-husbands demanding to talk to her. Sara Baxter and Jesus Sanchez, her partners in the kitchen on Mondays, gave her looks that said, we're glad it's you and not us. Not that Sara hadn't had her share of drama in life, or Jesus either. Sara had been a cook on a tugboat on the Mississippi and at an exclusive fishing camp in Alaska and for a real duke in England. She was living in Kansas City to be near her two grandchildren, whom she was absolutely crazy about. Jesus had come to Cafe Heaven through the placement program of the nearby Catholic Church. He had his green card and very good English skills, thanks to the U.S. government and the help he had provided them in Honduras and Nicaragua. Jesus had photos of himself in jungle camo gear holding a bazooka. He had lived Jumpin' Jack's wildest dreams.

"We're okay with the orders," Sara said. "You do what you have to do, we'll take care of the food."

Sara was pulling a pan of lamb shanks out of the

oven as she spoke. Jesus was arranging asparagus and blanched snow peas around a small ramekin of spicy peanut dip. Heaven sighed. She'd rather stay in the kitchen and cook.

But two ex-husbands in your face cannot be denied. Sandy Martin had been Heaven's childhood sweetheart, from ninth grade on. He was the son of Flint Hills ranchers and even though he wasn't in Kansas anymore he had kept the boots and leather vests and silver belt buckles for a sort of "courtroom cowboy" look. It worked well for him.

Big, sandy-haired and bearded, the men on the jury always took Sandy for the kind of guy you could watch a ball game with, share a six-pack. They might miss the fact that his cowboy boots cost a thousand dollars and he owned his own twin-engine Cessna.

The women on the jury saw something else. They saw a sexy man who was full of life and wasn't afraid to show some of his feelings. Sex appeal and cunning never hurt a bit with the women on the bench and on the other side of the aisle either.

Women knew Sandy might lead them down the garden path, but they went anyway. They knew it would be at the least, worth the trip.

If Sandy Martin was fire, Jason Kelley must be ice, Heaven mused, eying his immaculate black outfit. Jason was dark, elegant, sophisticated. Because he was a designer he showed his style in his appearance, hair smoothed back, clever belt, English shoes. He was European-looking, handsome, haughty. Heaven remembered with a twinge how warm and fun-loving Jason really was. Or could be. Or had been, before it all fell apart.

She jerked her head back to the present and away

from Jason. He was busy conferring with Sara about grilling quail.

"Sandy, I'll be right out. Don't even think of leaving before I meet your new . . . ?" Heaven left the question dangling.

"Associate, Katy, associate. Tasha is a new lawyer at the office. From New York City. A real shark in the courtroom." Sandy's face was peering through the pass-through. "You two are going to love each other."

"I can't wait!" Heaven snapped. "And now for you, Mr. Kelley. What brings you to this, your favorite hellhole?"

Jason had hated the restaurant, even if he had been all for the idea originally. To him it had destroyed a perfectly good relationship, stolen his playmate and been a bottomless pit for money. Of course, he was right. Still, Heaven did resent him standing there, right or not, munching blanched asparagus, looking amused and repulsed at the same time.

"I need to trade cars for the night, okay, H?"

Jason owned a great old bathtub-body MG. Heaven owned a van that doubled as Cafe Heaven's catering van. In the course of Jason's professional life as an architect who specialized in commercial interiors, he occasionally needed to haul something bigger than a bread box which ruled out the MG. This had been no problem when they were married, which they hadn't been for six months now.

"Sure, I don't think I'll ever leave here anyway. I've only been here for eleven hours. And the place is filling up with Monday night luminaries—Barbara and Hillary and the neighborhood mind police and two ex-husbands. Why would I want to be anywhere else?

"Please drive the little critter around by the back

door so I can keep an eye on it, though," she said. "Some desperate crack addict could put that tiny thing on the back of a pickup and take off with it. And I need the van for a catering job tomorrow. By eleven A.M., okay?"

"Yes, ma'am." Jason kissed her lightly on her sweaty brow and swatted her bottom on the way out the door.

Heaven took a deep breath and headed for the dining room.

One down and one to go.

Out in the cool darkness there was a traffic jam around the table of Sandy Martin and friend.

League ladies were lined up while the lovely Miss Tasha was nibbling on one of their triple chocolate delights; a waiter was pouring the last of a bottle of Franciscan Chardonnay, Oakville Estate, into their glasses, and Joe Long, aka Hillary, was passing out programs for tonight's show and glaring at the present-day Carrie Nations. Whenever he could, he flounced and made his blond pageboy wig fly.

Heaven decided to tackle the Fudge Patrol first. "Ladies, thank you so much for coming in this evening, but we try to *sell* desserts at this establishment. Why, I see at least seven or eight customers munching on your, ah, confections. Now, how am I going to make any money this way?" Heaven was trying the jovial I'm-just-a-simple-girl-from-Kansas ploy.

"We hope you will not make a dime. We have had the most distressing reports of these Monday night shows. Of profanity. Of sexual cross-gender-bendering. Of vulgar songs!"

The speaker was a severe woman in her early thirties. Her face was rigid with purpose. Behind her, like a choir behind a pulpit were the other three, considerably older, women warriors. All four were attired in cardigan sweaters buttoned to the neck, longish pleated skirts, sensible shoes. There was the hint of several layers of undergarments. Heaven surmised they felt even the tiniest show of skin could provoke the kind of thoughts they were out to squelch.

"Nonsense, ladies," Heaven cooed. "This is merely the fine American tradition of encouraging the creative arts, without which our fair community would wilt, would crumble, would lack the spark that ignites greatness in young minds."

Heaven knew it wasn't good but it was the best she could do right now. As if on cue, a group of six young minds walked by on their way to a table near the stage, accompanied by bodies clothed entirely in identical black leather. Not a creative thought between them. Great timing.

Heaven hurried on. "Ladies, we are merely exercising our first amendment rights to freedom of speech, a great American privilege."

The spokesperson spoke, eyes shining with fervor. "And we, Missy, will exercise that same right outside your establishment tonight in an effort to save these young people from the confusion and torment that you and your merry band of pranksters"—she gave a sidelong glare at Hillary and Barbara across the room—"have in store for them. Here, have some fudge!"

With that, the entourage swept out leaving Heaven holding a melting, gooey cube. She couldn't resist tasting it. Needed more vanilla.

"Loved your legal allusions, darling." Sandy's new associate gave Heaven a condescending smile. "I'd love to meet you in the courtroom sometime. Too bad you can't practice law anymore."

Heaven could feel the hairs on the back of her neck stand straight up. The witch had a lot of nerve insulting her on her own turf. She leaned down and grabbed the slim, bejeweled hand of this creature and quickly kissed it, then held the wrist tightly in her own strong grip.

"And it's so nice to meet you too, Tasha. I suppose my darling ex-husband told you that silly story about me being disbarred for being a drug lord in the seventies. That's a tale he tells to hide the real reason I was disbarred"—Heaven held delivery of her next line a beat for maximum drama—"manslaughter of a woman I caught in the wrong place at the wrong time."

With that, Heaven took the lovely hand of her ex-husband's new associate and knocked over the almost-full wineglass into Tasha's lap. Only then did she let go.

"Oh, my dear, you've gotten yourself all wet. I'll have Sam mop you up, and I think I'll send you an apple crisp on the house. That fudge must have left a bad taste in your mouth. Sandy, don't enjoy this too much, dear."

Sandy did seem to be enjoying himself but he suppressed out-and-out laughter and started drying Tasha off. "Don't believe a thing she said," he murmured.

As if on cue, and because he'd been watching in horror, Sam arrived to repair the damage. Joe and Chris descended for a conference. No time for reflection tonight, Heaven mused. I guess I'll just keep blundering forward.

"We decided," said Joe, with the glint of a mad genius in his eye, "that this little problem out front could be used to our advantage, publicitywise."

"So," finished Chris with the same missionary zeal that Heaven had just encountered in the League Fudge Patrol, "we've called all the television stations. And, of course, with my connections at least two of the three are on the way. Joe and I are going to start our Barbara and Hillary piece in front of the cafe. It will be on the *Ten O'clock News*. Great idea, huh?"

Chris *was* well-known to the media in Kansas City. He had been the victim of a severe beating, a gay bashing, several years before. Since then, he had become a gay activist in the art world. Chris wrote plays and performance art that usually had something to say about the gay experience. He had won several grants and prizes for his efforts and didn't really have to work as a waiter anymore. But he still did. Cafe Heaven was like a family, and Chris wasn't ready to leave home yet.

Heaven wished she saw this whole evening in the positive light Chris had tried to shine on it. She just wanted to go home. She went to the kitchen instead.

Chapter 4

The room was filling up, with people, with laughter, with the strains of Sarah Vaughn crooning from the sound system. It was 9:00 P.M. and the first act usually went on about 9:30. The tables were all occupied, some crammed with extra chairs that were kept in the basement the rest of the week.

In theory, everyone who sat down was supposed to eat, but Heaven had no stomach for enforcing dining room rules. The waiters, in an attempt to salvage tips that would bear some relation to the amount of people served, had instituted a five-dollar per person minimum. It was hard not to spend five-dollars when espresso was a dollar seventy-five and so was the popular local beer, Boulevard.

Nine o'clock also marked the arrival of the host for the evening, Murray Steinblatz. Murray was greatly loved by the Cafe Heaven crowd. He was also something of a legend around Kansas City.

Thirty-five years before, Murray had left Kansas City and the cramped quarters over his family's dry goods store. Up until then he had shared his life and a single bathroom with his grandmother Nadia, a survivor of Auschwitz, his parents and three sisters. The Steinblatz store was situated on Brooklyn Avenue. Brooklyn at Twenty-sixth Street was a neighborhood warily shared by Jewish immigrants from central and eastern Europe and black families inching their way toward the invisible DMZ zone of Kansas City, Troost Avenue. Troost was the street that was black on one side, white on the other in the 1990s. In the 1950s, it wasn't that clear-cut.

Murray went off to Columbia University on a scholarship to study journalism, staying with an aunt and uncle on the Upper West Side of Manhattan. He graduated, did his time writing obits at *Newsday* out on Long Island, then was hired as a crime reporter for the *New York Times*. Although the *Times* hated reporting on crime and would have avoided it entirely if possible, during Murray's stint it won them two Pulitzer prizes and lots of readers from the *Daily News*.

It was the best of both worlds.

Murray could rip your heart out with a phrase back then. He was cynical, witty, courageous and romantic all at the same time. He moved from day-to-day beat reporting to a three-times-a week column. The city was his.

Then one Wednesday evening in 1986 the fickle finger of fate pointed at Murray and took the city back. Murray and his wife, Eva, were walking to their Sheridan Square apartment. They'd been at the White Horse Tavern on Hudson having a bowl of chili and a beer. A car with three teenagers speeding from the scene of their latest holdup hit Eva as she crossed Christopher Street. The car tossed her in the air like an empty paper coffee cup. When she landed, her neck snapped and she was gone.

The kids were caught five blocks away when they ran the car into a traffic light pole. The car was stolen. They were under sixteen and never went to trial. And Murray never wrote another column about crime in the city.

He brought his wife's body back to Kansas City and buried her in Sheffield Cemetery, next to his sister Eileen. His parents and the dry goods store were history by then too.

For two years Murray didn't do much except walk around Loose Park on the jogging path. Then in 1989 when Cafe Heaven opened he asked Heaven for a job. Any job. He missed people, and he knew if he didn't start mixing in the stew of humanity again he would be lost forever.

So, on Mondays, Fridays and Saturdays Murray was the host, the maitre d', the front man for Cafe Heaven. On Mondays he even introduced the acts. Every week before he hit the small stage at the back of the room, Murray went to every table and said hello. He joked with the young folks, made someone's parents feel welcome, talked New York talk to a table of four from Brooklyn. By the time the show started he knew the lay of the land, who to play to and where the troublemakers were lurking.

Tonight the trouble outside was making Murray twitchy.

"I can't help it, Murray," Heaven said. "They won't go away tonight. So the guys decided to make the best of it. They've called the stations and they're going to do Barb and Hillary out on the street. All we can hope is that it reads as clever political satire and not a drag queen contest." Heaven was stirring three orders of red wine risotto as she spoke.

Risotto with Mushrooms and Asparagus

1 lb. assorted mushrooms: crimini, shitake, oyster (or a combination of standard white mushrooms and dried morels or porcini soaked in warm water one hour)
1 lb. asparagus
1 small onion, chopped very fine
1 lb. arborio rice
olive oil and butter
2 qt. liquids, half should be chicken stock but the rest can be either wine, mushroom liquid, or vegetable stock. In this case we are using a red Italian wine, Barbera D'Alba
1/2 cup Parmesan cheese, the best you can afford, salt and white pepper to taste.

Saute mushrooms in a little olive oil and butter and set aside. Blanch asparagus by a quick dip in boiling water until they turn bright green. Then plunge them in a bowl of ice water. Just running cold water over them won't do. Chop off the tips and three or four inches of stalk. Save the rest for soup.

With a low flame under the heaviest saucepan or saute pan you have: Saute onion in a butter/ oil combo until clear. Add rice and coat the grains with the oil.

After a couple of minutes start adding liquid a little at a time, just enough to cover the rice.

Stir often with a wooden spoon. Alternate chicken stock and the wine or other liquid.

Continue adding the liquids a little at a time. The rice is done when it is still firm at the very middle of the grain but not crunchy to the taste.

This takes about 25 minutes. When it reaches this stage, add the mushrooms, a tablespoon of butter, the cheese, the salt and pepper, and the sections of asparagus, saving the tips to decorate the top of the dish.

"Okay, kid, but I don't have a good feeling about this one." Murray squirmed and threw a handful of pecans in his mouth.

"It doesn't seem to be stopping anyone from coming in." Heaven glanced up at the long line of order tickets.

"I think I'll play it like it's all part of a big new performance piece, whataya think?" Murray asked no one in particular.

Sara looked up from the grill where she was working on four pork tenderloins and a couple of quail. "Get outta here, Murray, you bother me."

"It's my animal magnetism, babe."

As Murray hit the swinging OUT door of the kitchen, Sam hit the swinging IN door.

"Heaven, you'd better come out here. There's something the matter with that chick that's with your ex. I don't know if she got real drunk or what but she says her throat hurts, and I think she was sick in the bathroom. Now she can't walk very well. Your ex says she just needs air but I don't know."

Heaven and Sam grabbed Murray away from a table and maneuvered their way through the bar crowd toward the front door. Outside the 39th Street League of Decency marched resolutely, handing out fudge to latecomers and admonishing everyone to stay out in the fresh air. Across the street, Channel 9 and Channel 5 had set up cameras with portable lights all aglow. Sandwiched in between the cameras and the protesters, Hillary and Barb were exchanging recipes and plastic hydrogen bombs and wicked, wet kisses.

The trio made it to the doorway just in time to see Tasha fall from the grip of Sandy Martin onto the pavement. There was an inert look to her body. As Heaven and Sam and Murray and Barb and Hillary hurried toward the still form someone rushed out of the cafe and pushed them roughly aside. Camouflage blurred by.

"Take cover," Jumpin' Jack yelled as he dove on Tasha's limp body. "They'll be back. Duck! Hold your breath! It's Agent Orange! It's napalm! It's our boys!"

It was 9:30. The show had begun.

Chapter 5

"Okay, Heaven. It's your turn. Bring me some hot coffee and get your ass over here." Detective Bonnie Weber lit another cigarette and looked around the dining room.

It was after two in the morning. The picket line, television crews and audience had all been sent on their way. Joe, Chris, Sam and the rest of the staff had been interviewed and were drinking beer at the bar. Sara and Jesus had put in their two cents worth and had gone back to the kitchen to help the dishwasher finish up. Jumpin' Jack had been sent to Western Missouri Mental Health for a checkup and Murray Steinblatz had reluctantly gone home.

Bonnie slipped her shoes off. She was making some progress. Two hundred potential suspects down and only one more to go. Saving the best for last.

The best and the hardest.

It was always difficult to question someone you know.

In the summer of 1971, Bonnie and Heaven had taken college courses together. They had been lab partners in criminal evidence. Bonnie was finishing up her degree and Heaven was brushing up to get ready for law school in the fall. They had even gone to law school together until Bonnie had walked out of first year torts and driven directly to sign up for the police academy. She was now the first woman detective assigned to homicide in Kansas City police history.

"You know, Bonnie, the woman could have died from perfectly natural causes," Heaven said defensively as she poured coffee. "And if, just if, she didn't die of natural causes, there must have been at least a dozen people that had access to her food and drink, including those zealots from the Thirty-ninth Street League. They were handing out candy right and left." Heaven paused and frowned. "I even ate a piece."

"Right, and you look just fine to me," murmured Detective Weber, pouring sugar and cream in her fresh cup of Heaven blend, a mix of espresso, Colombian and Kenya AA.

"It could have been an enemy from New York. She was a prosecutor in Queens, according to Sandy. Some Colombian drug lord could have sent someone out here to do her with a fucking poison dart or something."

"Right." Bonnie lit another Marlboro Light.

"I just don't know why you had to come in here like the fucking Gestapo and interrogate everybody, including Dave Eckert from Channel Nine, for God's sake!"

"Yes, you do know why." Bonnie stared evenly across the table at Heaven. "You know exactly why. Because by the time the coroner establishes the cause of death it will be impossible to re-create this intimate little gathering, won't it? As it is, most of the physical evidence was destroyed by the busboys. Plates cleaned and leftovers in the garbage. Garbage in the Dumpster. Wine bottle pitched, wineglasses washed. Very tidy joint you got here, old friend."

"How was the busboy to know? How were any of us to know?" Heaven snapped, slamming down a glass of Haywood Zinfandel she was drinking from.

"Okay, let's start from the top. Monday nights are open mike night, right? And tonight the two fags were doing some kind of drag act, and the old biddies got wind of it and swooped down on you, right?"

"Gosh, Bonnie, I couldn't have put it better myself," Heaven answered in a voice laden with sarcasm.

"You ever had a run-in with the League before?"

"Never. As a matter of fact, we're on their side when it comes to the Diamond Theater. We were very upset when our neighborhood slum lord, Rodriquez, rented the old place to the Three Stooges."

Heaven was referring to the three brothers Spelling, who owned a string of porno stores and topless bars in the Kansas City area.

"All the restaurants and shops went together and signed a letter of protest and hand delivered it to Rodriquez. The biker bar even signed it. We don't mind a little sleaze here on Thirty-ninth, but we don't want hard-core smut. We've all worked too hard." Heaven's voice had taken on a desperate edge.

She took a deep breath and closed her eyes tightly. Like she could then open them and make the day go away, like it could be nine in the morning again and the only thing broken would be the dishwashing machine. She opened her eyes and went on.

"I know it's hard to understand, but what we do here, the bad and the good of it, is not to satisfy prurient interests. If someone uses the word *fuck* in a poem or someone hangs from the ceiling in a go-go cage or sings a song about the mayor, well, I'd like to say it's all art but that would be pushing it. It is all in the interest of the creative process." Heaven was perking up.

"Right." Bonnie Weber knew she had to listen even though she ached for a long, hot bath. She thought about her husband, Ed, and the kids sawing logs at home. She wanted to wrap this up.

"So the fags in drag and that stuff is all for art but somehow the League ladies misunderstood and came down here and started raising hell and then your guys called the media to get a free hit on the *Ten O'clock News*. I think I've got that part. You wanna tell me about the ex and the broad? And, by the way, what was this other ex of yours, Jason Kelley, doing at their table?"

"Jason? You're kidding? What would he be talking to Sandy about?"

"It was the broad. He was talking to the broad says Sam. The lawyer had gone to the john and the other one had just come in and made a beeline for their table, so the story goes. She doing it with two of your gently used boyfriends, H?"

"Husbands, Bonnie, gently used husbands. I'm sure Sam must have been mistaken. Maybe Jason was talking to the table next to them. I've never seen her before in my life, I swear. Come to think of it, I haven't seen either one of the "ex's" in weeks. Jason couldn't know her. She's new in Sandy's office. Or she was." Heaven couldn't believe this was happening. She was even getting confused about which ex she was talking about. It was all too much. Customers were not supposed to drop dead. Especially not pretty ones who provoke semiviolence before they die.

"What'd they eat?"

"Duck burritos, then Sandy had a lamb shank and she had the risotto. But I didn't even know it was for them when I made it."

"What about the apple crisp you sent out to them after you threatened her life?" Bonnie asked calmly.

"Threaten? Why that's ridiculous! That little bitch was in my face about how I can't practice law anymore so I told her some stupid tale about . . ." Heaven's voice trailed off as she recalled exactly what she did say. "About manslaughter, I guess. I get it. She pisses me off, and I send her a poison apple, just like the wicked stepmother, only in this case it's the wicked ex-wife."

"Right." Bonnie sighed. "You were seen grabbing her wrist in an aggressive manner and spilling a glass of wine on her."

"I guess no one mentioned that I also kissed her hand? Come on, Bonnie, you know I can be an asshole. I'm too old to be pushed by some gorgeous babe lawyer and an ex-husband.

"How did I know my deed would come back to haunt me so soon? Would I have been so obvious if I had slipped her a Mickey, for Christ's sake?"

"People do funny things, Heaven. Why you yourself took a perfectly good career and stuffed it down the toilet ten years ago. How do I know this isn't another of your once-in-a-decade mistakes?"

Detective Bonnie Weber stood up and stretched.

"But, hell, the coroner is probably going to tell us

that she keeled of a massive stroke. Or something. But I don't think so. The medical examiner was pretty excited for it to be a heart attack. I'm outta here. I'll call you."

Bonnie stopped at the door. "Heaven? I gotta tell you, don't stray too far from the stove. As in, don't leave town."

Chapter 6

It was almost three in the morning when Heaven pointed Jason's MG north on Southwest Trafficway. Unlike most of her friends she didn't live around the fashionable Country Club Plaza area of Kansas City.

Twenty-two years before, Heaven returned to Kansas City pregnant from a brief marriage to an English rock musician and a brief residency in London. A friend who worked at City Hall treated her to a welcome back lunch at Lucien's, a now-defunct Italian restaurant in the Columbus Park neighborhood of downtown Kansas City. After lunch they explored the streets and Heaven found herself in front of a roomy flat with a FOR RENT sign stuck in the window. It became home for Heaven and soon for her baby daughter, Iris.

She and Iris were befriended by Angelo Broncato, eighty-six, who lived and had his bakery in the building next door. When Angelo died with no family in America, he surprised the whole neighborhood by leaving his building to Heaven. Heaven used to say it was the only good thing a man had ever given her.

One day after making that crack she felt ashamed. How whiny and bitter you sound, girl! And you have Iris so it isn't even true. Don't whine like that anymore, she told herself.

No matter where fate had led her she had always had the bakery to return to. Eventually. The downstairs space gradually became a catering kitchen and prep area. The big coal ovens that Angelo had used to bake bread were not functional anymore but they lent an air of history to the kitchen. You knew that people had been receiving sustenance from the place long before Heaven started cooking there. There was plenty of room in the basement for a darkroom. Both Heaven and Iris indulged in black-and-white photography. The second-floor living quarters had evolved over the years. There were fewer rooms as Heaven knocked out unnecessary partitions.

Fewer walls but lots more stuff: paintings, antique quilts, Zapotec rugs, Arts and Crafts movement furniture, her beloved jukebox. Heaven was a pack rat.

The neighborhood had evolved too.

Columbus Park was always the immigrants first stop in Kansas City. The Irish of the 1880s had been gradually replaced by the Italians in the 1910s. For many years it remained a staunchly Italian neighborhood.

About the same time Heaven moved into the neighborhood, in the 1970s, a large influx of Vietnamese arrived. Holy Rosary, the Catholic Church that was the heart of the community, had sponsored a hundred Catholic Viet families forced to flee when the South fell. Instead of one hundred, two hundred families showed up. Their religious affiliation did not give them good survival chances under the new Communist regime. So Viet dialects mingled with Sicilian and midwestern twangs on the streets of Columbus Park.

Heaven drove the MG into the garage she had built over Angelo's parking lot. It had a door that led upstairs so Heaven didn't have to go to the outside entrance when she came home at three in the morning.

In no time she was out of her clothes and under the shower trying to dissolve the knot of tension between her shoulders with the shower head on the "torture" setting.

If only I hadn't been so stupid and let that woman get to me, Heaven thought. If I had just thought before I made that crack about manslaughter. If only I'd had the sense to say no to the TV cameras. If only Tasha had a tragic but deadly disease.

Heaven was afraid that wasn't going to be the case. This was going to be murder. For everyone.

As she eased into an oversized white terry robe, she heard the doorbell ring.

If I had a lick of sense I'd just pretend I didn't hear a thing. But it's too late for sense tonight. Heaven had this dialog with herself as she went downstairs and through the dark kitchen. When she looked through the peephole she instantly started crying.

Heaven opened the door.

"You silly boy, you'll never get to be a doctor if you stay up half the night waiting for me to get home. You should be in bed." Heaven grabbed the sleeve of Huy Wing, better known to his American friends as Hank.

Hank had come to America from Vietnam with his mother and older sister when he was four. They had eighty-six U.S. dollars and the clothes on their backs. Hank's father had been killed a week before they arrived in Kansas City, suspected of being a U.S.A.

sympathizer, which he was. Twenty years later, Hank's sister was doing graduate work at MIT and Hank was in his first year of residency at the Kansas University Medical Center.

He was going to be a heart surgeon.

He was tall and good-looking, dark eyes flashing, long black hair pulled back in a ponytail.

He was only four years older than Iris, Heaven's daughter.

He was crazy about Heaven.

"Hey, I'm the young one remember. I can stay up half the night and still be fine the next morning. It's folks your age who need their rest." Hank's voice was full of teasing and affection. Then he noticed the tears. "Oh, Heaven, I was just kidding."

He kissed each eyelid with such tender gravity. It made Heaven feel her heart would stop beating. After closing the door and locking the locks Heaven put her back against the wall and sank. As she melted to the floor she grabbed Hank's hand.

"It's not you. It's the entire rest of the world."

Heaven started with the exhaust hood and ended with Detective Bonnie Weber. Hank sat beside her on the floor, touching, kissing, listening. When she finished he stood up and pulled her up beside him.

"Then we'd better go to bed. You've got to start catering in five hours. And I've got rounds in four." Hank pushed her hair out of her eyes. "Don't lose heart, Heaven. You're innocent. Everything will be fine."

Heaven had always been a sucker for a man who knew how to lie.

Chapter 7

When Heaven hit the back door of the restaurant, it was 9:30 A.M. and she was late.

"I'm sorry, guys," she groaned. "Could you read all of my instructions and checklists for the catering food?"

"No problem, boss. We didn't expect you this soon. We heard." Pauline Kramer, the baker, spoke as she bent over the counter, shaping bread dough into loaves. Pauline herself looked a lot like Olive Oil, Popeye's cartoon girlfriend. She was a beanpole with a mop of black hair and big feet and a gangly grace about her movements. She could bake the best chocolate cake, the flakiest fruit tarts, the crispiest cookie. But her real love was baking bread. She looked up with apprehension.

"In fact, I caught it live, on Channel Nine," Brian Hoffman, who was chopping red peppers with lightning speed, said with a smirk. "Boy, when you call the media, you give 'em a show. I loved the part where the chick fell in a heap. Very realistic, man." Brian smoked a lot of pot.

"Gee, Brian, I'm so glad you liked it. Unfortunately this was not art, honey. She really did die right in front of our humble cafe," Heaven said.

"Whoa, man, rude dude." Brian was impressed.

Heaven scanned the prep list and poured herself a cup of coffee. "It looks like you have this under control. I'm going to hit Sal's to see what the neighborhood buzz is." Out the back door, down the alley, across the street to Sal's she trudged.

Much like a small town barbershop, Sal's was the communication center for the neighborhood. Sal had been cutting hair right there for forty years. The mayor stopped in once a week, art students waited beside retired postmen who waited next to waiters from the city's trendiest spots. And every one of them left a little piece of information with Sal. So-and-so was seen dining with their divorce lawyer again, an amendment was in trouble and was not going to be passed in City Council, the fifties store had a whole estate of great Haywood Wakefield furniture. Sal took every piece of information and buffed it up a little and sent it on its way. To say Sal had his finger on the pulse of Thirty-ninth Street would be an understatement.

"Okay, Sal, give it to me straight. I'm a big girl, I can take it." Heaven started talking the moment she hit the door and quickly flung herself in the chrome and Naugahyde chair nearest Sal's stool. Mona Kirk, owner of the "City Cat" store was in Sal's too, in the chair by the window, drinking coffee and watching Heaven with a look of anticipation. As the owner of one of the first cat stores in the country, Mona always tried to wear the latest in cat glamour. Today she was sporting rhinestone whisker earrings, several narrow wires strung with sparkles that stood out on each side of her head and from each ear at least three inches. That, along with her short gray haircut, one of Sal's variations on the crew cut, made it hard to keep eyes off Mona above the neck. Her store didn't open until ten, and she always stopped by Sal's first to get the morning news.

"Oh, doll, I almost had to call you at home. I didn't think I could wait another minute to hear the news. I knew you needed your rest, though. Poor baby," Mona said in a very insincere tone. She could hardly wait to get the niceties out of the way and get to the good stuff.

"Well, babe, you've done it this time." Sal smiled without stopping the neck trim he was working on or dropping the unlit cigar he clenched between his teeth. Sal knew he had the floor and Mona would have to wait. After all, it was his joint.

"I'd say about half the neighborhood thinks the broad was knocked off by you in a rage of some kind. The word is out you threw a drink on her."

"Not exactly," Heaven started her defense but Sal turned and gave her a look. She shut up in a pout.

"Another, say . . . thirty percent think it's her mysterious past as a drug dealer mouthpiece in the Big Apple."

"She wasn't, she was a prosecutor . . ." Heaven tried again and this time both Mona and Sal gave her the look. Mona was enjoying hearing what everyone else thought. This would save lots of phone time later in the morning.

Sal continued. "Then there are all kinds of wild stories. 'She's an actress you paid, and she's not really dead.' 'It's a conspiracy against the neighborhood,' you know. Any press is bad press, that kinda thing. Another theory is that Jumpin' Jack really works for the FBI, he injected her with a lethal shot 'cause she knew too much." Sal paused and chuckled. "About what, nobody is quite sure."

"Caught the whole thing myself on Channel Five," Sal continued. "Loved the Thirty-ninth Street Rockettes out in front with the candy. That Helen McDermott, she'd be a handsome woman if she'd take off that damn long skirt, show a little leg."

Sal had given this instant poll complete with percentages and guest commentary without missing a snip of the scissors. Now he paused and studied his friend, and for the first time saw the worry in her eyes.

"Aw, kid, don't take it so hard. She probably croaked of some natural thing, ya know? So what if she was young and eh, healthy looking. It was probably a heart attack. Yeah, a heart attack. She's a lawyer. Lottsa pressure. Nobody really blames you. Honest."

Sal was brushing off the neck of the elderly man in his chair who was in turn eying Heaven like she was Lizzie Borden.

"Yeah, Sal, I hope Bonnie calls soon with the autopsy reports. I hope it is a heart attack. I could use some good news." Heaven stared vacantly across the street. Mona was afraid Heaven would leave before they got all the gossip so she swung into action.

"I stopped for gas and Bernie said he heard it was food poisoning," Mona offered cheerfully.

"Great, Mona. Either I'm guilty of a crime of passion or professional negligence, depending on what block you're standing on.

"Sal, Mona, here's the little bit of truth I know. I

had never seen the victim before last night." Heaven felt herself break into a sweat when she said the word *victim*. "She was with my first husband, Sandy. You met Sandy last year at my New Years Day party. Yes, the . . . Tasha, and I did have a little good-natured competitive oratory. But I did not knock her off. I don't have a clue what or who did. Spread the word, please, Sal?"

With that, Heaven got up, hugged Mona and before anyone could get another question out, slammed the door and headed back across the street, leaving Sal and Mona in possession of "straight from the horse's mouth" information. She hoped it would help.

Heaven went back to work in the kitchen. There was lots to do and she welcomed the chance to chop and dice, to focus on something besides the calamity of the night before. She actually managed to shift her attention to the salad she was creating and enjoy the kitchen. Pauline was slicing goat cheese tarts into squares. Brian was grilling hundreds of chicken and pork strips. Everyone was quiet, probably because all they really wanted to do was talk about what had happened the night before. Somehow, however, they knew Heaven needed a break from questions.

An hour later the food was almost ready to depart. The crew discussed where to put what in the van and started loading bread in big plastic carriers and the salads in coolers and insulated containers. The door of the kitchen opened. Bonnie Weber and her partner, Harry Stein, walked in. The looks on their faces were grim.

Heaven looked pleadingly at her old friend. She couldn't say a word, her vocal cords were frozen. No one else said anything either. Brian and Pauline had not met the detectives the night before but they weren't stupid. They could spot a cop when one or two walked in the back door.

"H, the only thing worse would have been a smoking gun with your prints on it. She was poisoned," Bonnie said.

"Oh, shit!" Brian, Pauline and Heaven said more or less at the same time.

"Nicotine poisoning to be exact," Bonnie continued. "She had ingested so many different things the doc doesn't know yet where it came from. More tests, stuff sent off to the regional lab, in time we'll know more."

"Nicotine? Did someone smoke themself to death?" Jason Kelley came in the back door dangling the keys to the van in his hand.

"Bonnie, this is Jason Kelley. We spoke of him last night. Jason, shut up and listen." Heaven felt like Alice in the rabbit hole.

Harry Stein was slowly circling the kitchen, picking up jars of spices and opening them, sniffing. "The doc says the stuff is very lethal, that it's an alkaloid, that it only takes forty milligrams to kill ya. That's the amount in just two cigarettes. Course the nicotine burns off when you light a cigarette. The doc also said it's used by gardeners to kill rose aphids. Nicotine is. The doc's a gardener himself."

"You think you're going to find some ground up Camels in one of the jars, Harry?" Heaven asked, bristling. Harry Stein always rubbed Heaven the wrong way. He was a skinny, wiry guy with a mean sense of humor. Before he made it to homicide, Harry had been in burglary in Midtown and had come to the Thirty-ninth Street Neighborhood Association meetings a couple of times to lecture on safeguarding your home or business. He once told them they sure didn't have much to steal on Thirty-ninth Street. Heaven couldn't see how Bonnie worked with such a jerk.

"Naw, H, you wouldn't be that dumb." Harry sneered. "Of course, you've been dumb before."

"Look, guys, I didn't even know nicotine was a separate thing. I certainly don't know where you get the stuff."

"Heaven, you do know about the big three, motive, means, opportunity, though doncha? You learned about them in law school, I bet." Harry continued circling. "Motive, I think it might be a little thin but you *did* make a scene with the woman. You're jealous your ex and the dame were cozy last night."

Jason reacted. He couldn't help it. He looked guilty for just a moment. Then he realized who Harry Stein was talking about. The look Jason sent across the room to Heaven then said, how could you be jealous of another man? Heaven felt defensive, like she had just been caught doing something naughty. But she had caught the first, fleeting expression on Jason's face. So had Harry Stein.

"What dame? What happened?" Jason was definitely losing his usual cool, there was a thin line of sweat on his upper lip.

"Haven't you seen the tube, man?" Brian piped in. "It was awesome. This chick croaked right outside the place, man. The TV cameras were here, and the whole thing was like a scene from a flick, man."

Bonnie eyed Jason with new interest. "Yeah, he's summed it all up beautifully. The woman with Sandy Martin died. Tasha Arnold. You must have seen them last night. You were here last night?"

"I only saw Sandy. I came right to the kitchen and I went out the back door," Jason murmured through clenched teeth. He was not taking this news well. Bonnie made a mental note of the discrepancy between his story and the wait staff version.

Harry continued his spiel directed at Heaven. "Opportunity, you bet. The poison could have been slipped in the wine or the water or any of the food items.

"All we need is the means to have a great little murder case against you. Of course, Sandy Martin defends you, says you were just being a bitch, not a killer. Which is it, Heaven?" Harry finished his speech and his tour of the kitchen and looked at Heaven smugly.

Jason stared at Heaven with shock and dismay in his face. The kitchen staff stared at Harry Stein like he had just grown two heads. Heaven stared helplessly at Bonnie as if she were the last lifeboat on a sinking cruise ship.

Bonnie was stuck between her real affection for Heaven and the case she wanted to solve. Maybe she should take herself off this one. But she couldn't throw Heaven to the dogs, or in this case, to Harry Stein.

Bonnie broke the uneasy silence. "You could be right, H, what you said last night. The victim had only been in Kansas City a couple months. It could be revenge from some case she was involved with in New York. I've already started that line of investigation. I hope I get something. In the meantime . . ." Bonnie's voice trailed off.

"I guess I should have known something terrible would happen when you were both in here at once,"

Heaven moaned as she walked toward Jason. "I should never let any of my ex-husbands come near this place. It's clearly disaster for me." She grabbed the keys out of Jason's hand and gave him his. His hand was shaking.

"What's the matter with you, Jason? You're a mess. Be useful and carry something out. Everybody grab something. I'm going to be late if I don't leave in three minutes. Help me," Heaven snapped as she grabbed a huge plastic container of salad.

As the crew arranged the food and coolers filled with wine and bottled water in the vans, Bonnie, Harry, Jason and Heaven stood by the MG.

"Heaven," Jason said, "I'm sorry I didn't stay around for the show last night. It turned out to be one of your best, I mean worst. Sorry, Detective. I'm making bad jokes because I'm nervous. Heaven, I'm sorry about the, eh, death. Thanks for letting me borrow the van." Little trickles of sweat were running down the side of Jason's face from his hairline. He looked down at the pavement and kicked at a clump of dirt.

Because the top on the MG was up, Jason jerked open the passenger side door to throw in his brief-case. As the door flew open, an amber bottle came rolling out onto the ground. It landed with a little ping but didn't break. Behind it a piece of paper flut-tered to the pavement like a feather. But all eyes were on the bottle. It was empty. The label on it read Black Leaf 40 Nicotine Sulfate. Poison. Detective Bonnie Weber reached down, and without touching anything but the edge, flipped over the piece of paper. It was a note that read: *"Heaven. I did what you asked. Your wish is still my command."*

Chapter 8

"I can't believe they let us go out on this gig." Sara Baxter sat next to Heaven in the van. She had shown up at work about the same time the empty nicotine bottle had shown up.

Now Heaven was white as a ghost, with tear streaks on her cheeks. "I guess my bursting into tears and groveling helped. After all, my life is probably ruined but the mayor still needs his lunch."

"Thank God Jason was there to explain the note," Heaven said. "Or try to. He seemed more freaked out than anyone. Damn, why didn't I see that note last night? I would have thrown it away. There would have been one less piece of the puzzle for that Harry Stein to fit together."

"I got the impression Bonnie's partner would love it if you and Jason were in cahoots," Sara said bluntly.

"I got that same impression. I guess it would make good press. I can just see the headline now, Ex Kills for Cafe Cutey."

"How can you alliterate at a time like this?" Sara

shook her head. "H, this all sucks. Whoever killed whatshername must have put that bottle in Jason's car so you'd look, you know . . ." Sara's voice trailed off and she stared out the van window.

"Now all we have to do is figure out who hates me that much." Heaven was already mentally compiling the short list.

"Do you think that group of fun-loving women that I asked to leave last week because they told Sam he had shit for brains, do you think they could have retaliated so fast?"

"Heaven, this is serious! Why would someone want to make you look so . . . guilty? Just when everything was going so well."

"That part is weird, isn't it? Things had been going pretty darn good. I was able to pay the sales tax and make payroll and repair the air conditioner all in the same two-week period. This poison thing can't be good for business. Of course there will be the ghouls. Maybe we should print a special menu. Tempt Fate. Defy the Odds. Eat the Same Meal Tasha Ate."

"Heaven, that's sick."

"I'm afraid sightseers are the best we can hope for this week." Heaven's voice quivered as she pulled up to the site of their lunch.

The former stockyards are one of Kansas City's most famous ghosts. A sprawling patch of bottom-land near the Kaw and Missouri rivers, the pungent smell of the slaughterhouse used to cause travelers to hold their breath as they crossed from Missouri to Kansas on the Lewis and Clark Viaduct above. Row after row of narrow wooden chutes led the fat China Poland pigs and the Black Angus cattle from the Flint Hills of Kansas down the path to the sledgehammer, then to the plants of lard renderers or bologna makers or wholesale beef companies.

With the exception of part of the wooden chutes connected to a small museum, it was all gone now. Most of the holding pens had been dismantled. The rendering plants and hot dog factories were long closed, moved close to the large feed lots in the middle of cattle and hog country.

A new cultural, residential community was being launched on the spot where cowboys used to roam. The city fathers were planning loft apartments in the turn-of-the-century buildings. They had chosen a developer that had experience in other cities with historic redevelopment. The first wave of shops and art galleries and restaurants was opening.

A sculpture park to honor the city's agricultural past had been commissioned. The bronze horse honoring the American Royal was in place. A tribute to the stockyards was still in the planning stages with the Municipal Arts Commission in a search mode for the right artist. A tribute to the wheat and grain business, a three-story breadbasket created by the international artist Ismaroldo Antonio was being dedicated today.

The burnished aluminum basket was filled with bronze wheat sheaves and polyurethane loaves of bread in bright colors. A riot of materials.

For the unveiling ceremonies two large cranes were poised to pull off the Christo-like tarp. A platform had been built for speech givers and a tent temporarily erected for a celebratory lunch. The lunch was not for the general public but an invited affair for the city council, arts commission, cultural elite. Heaven and her crew had cooked for two hundred.

As she and Sara started unloading the van, waiters hired for the event began to pull up in the parking lot, grabbing a box or cooler out of the van and heading for the tent. No one mentioned the television extravaganza of the night before. To Heaven at least. That is until Nolan Wilkins, the mayor's aide, made a beeline for her.

"Hey, darling, glad you're here. The speeches start in an hour, at twelve-thirty. Should take about forty-five minutes or an hour. The head of the Missouri Council for the Arts will lead it off, then the mayor, the developer, and, of course, Ismaroldo."

Suddenly Nolan looked around nervously. "Could I talk to you privately?" He steered Heaven away by the elbow.

"You know all the media will be here, Heaven, everybody and his brother. And, well, after last night, I wondered if you might keep a low profile today. We want the focus on the art and the artist not . . . well, your problem. You know I trust you, darling, but maybe you could just set up the tables and split? Before twelve-thirty?"

"Nolan, this is not the set of *Arsenic and Old Lace* for God's sake. These people have eaten my food dozens of times." Heaven could feel the heat in her cheeks. This hurt. "Shit, it's your nickel. I'll make it look cute and leave. Sara can stay and hold down the fort. They probably wouldn't eat if they saw me anyway."

"Thanks, darling. And don't think for a minute I think you killed that woman. After all, with all the ex husbands you have, you can't go around knocking off everyone they go out with. No one could. I mean . . ." Nolan's eyes started darting hopefully toward the speech platform, looking for escape.

"Nolan, stop while we're still on speaking terms." Heaven wheeled toward the tent.

To get everyone fed and back to running the city by two o'clock, Heaven had decided to go with two serving lines heading in opposite directions from a seventy-two-inch round table for the centerpiece. The theme of the sculpture had given Heaven great ideas for decorating the tables.

Long loaves of French bread had been dyed with bright food coloring and baskets had been sprayed with silver paint to simulate aluminum. Of course there were sheaves of wheat sprayed bronze. She placed the baskets filled with purple, hot pink and marigold colored bread loaves at various levels by propping them up underneath the tablecloth with bricks and milk crates. The wheat sheaves were also tied with bright colored ribbons that matched the bread. Then she arranged large monstera leaves around the perimeter of the table.

Pauline had really outdone herself on the bread actually meant for consumption. There was a beautiful red pepper bread, crusty lympa rye and a cottage cheese dill loaf that Heaven was especially fond of. These were spilling out of baskets and arranged on cutting boards so that waiters could slice to order later. There were crocks of whipped herb butter for slathering.

The rest of the food was to be arranged down both long tables. Everything was designed to be served at room temperature. Heaven didn't like to use those ugly industrial chafing dishes if she could help it. She took two of the round rye loaves and used them as giant pin cushions for skewers of flattened chicken breasts and strips of pork tenderloins that had been marinated Indonesian style and grilled. Around the bread loaves she laid blanched asparagus, making the whole dish resemble a giant flower, the skewers holding forth like stamen ready for a bee. Nestled in the middle of the arrangement she slipped a glass bowl filled with a peanut-sesame dipping sauce for both the meats and the asparagus.

Sara Baxter was filling three huge terra-cotta bowls with three salads. The first was a cucumber, lentil and feta combination tossed with a dijon vinaigrette. Then came a jicama Waldorf salad with grapes and oranges, followed by a multigrain extravaganza featuring barley, wheatberries and two kinds of rice. Sara was arranging artichoke hearts and plump pink shrimp on top of the grains.

Heaven moved on down the line and started arranging squares of a goat cheese and caramelized onion tart on long, irregular slabs of marble. Two of the servers were making artful piles with small shortcakes next to a giant glass bowl filled with a strawberry-rhubarb compote for dessert. There was another, only slightly less giant bowl of whipped cream.

It was, after all, spring in the midwest. The menu celebrated the heartland and the grains they were there to canonize.

Jicama Waldorf Salad

1 large or 2 medium jicamas
6 celery stalks, sliced
2 cups pecan halves, toasted

2 cups green seedless grapes, halved and
   pitted
6 oranges, peeled and diced
1 large container plain yogurt
honey
lime juice

You have a choice of grating the jicama with
the grater on your food processor or chopping it
up, apple style. Combine all the ingredients, season the yogurt with honey and lime juice to taste
and toss it all together.

Heartland Grain Salad

2 cups each, cooked wheatberries, wild
rice, barley and basmati rice
2 cups toasted seeds and nuts: some combination of pumpkin seeds, sesame seeds, sun-
flower seeds, peanuts, hazelnuts or cashews.
2 cups dried fruits: some combination of
apricots, dates, figs, raisins or prunes.
1 bunch parsley, finely chopped
Kosher salt and pepper
1 cup good olive oil or hazelnut oil
1/2 cup vinegar, balsamic or raspberry

Combine all the ingredients and let set over
night. Adjust the seasonings and dressing before
serving. You may need more of both dressing
and seasonings. Top with boiled and peeled
shrimp, artichoke hearts and some dried fruit

and nuts. Or arrange grilled chicken breasts cut into strips in a pinwheel design.

Heaven placed a last few strategic wheat stalks around for decoration and then yelled for attention. The troops gathered.

"Okay, everybody. Look at the first serving line and help Sara make the other one look just like it. You've got twenty minutes till speech time, then another forty-five or an hour till they stampede. Black plastic plates and black plastic silverware that's already rolled up in black paper napkins goes in the blank spot nearest the skewers. We have San Pelligrino for sparkling water and Mountain Valley water for still water. The wine is La Vielle Ferme blanc which you all probably know by now is a French from Rhone, very tasty for the price. But no tasting until after the gig is over. No smoking until then either.

"When they start the speeches you can start filling the glasses with water and wine. You've got three stations for beverages and I want the guests to be able to swoop in as soon as the unveiling is over and start swilling wine. The city is paying by the bottle today, kids.

"And speaking of the city, they have this funny idea that having their guests spot me here, after last night, would not be cool. So, I'm outta here. Sara, call when you're done, and I'll pick you up. Or I'll send someone else."

"What if someone asks who did the catering?" Eddie, one of the servers, was always promoting Heaven's catering.

"Just hand them a card quietly. Don't let my name

out of your mouth. We don't want panic among the art mob. It could get ugly."

Of course, to Heaven, it was already ugly. Being asked to leave your own gig, having someone die at your cafe, finding very incriminating evidence in the car you'd been driving, it seemed as ugly as a bad anxiety dream, where there are no solutions, only more problems.

As she pulled the van out of the parking lot the scared, lost kid inside her finally pushed aside the practical businesswoman. She could feel sorry for herself in the privacy of her own car. She'd give herself twenty minutes. Panic ensued.

This might be the worst, she muttered to herself. Banned. At least in 1982 you had no one to blame but yourself. You knew who had caused the mess. But now the idea that an unknown someone might be trying to discredit Cafe Heaven had taken shape. If that was the point, it had worked. Her client, this time the city, didn't want people to know she was responsible for the food they were eating. But the fact that the victim was with her ex-husband made it seem much more personal. How could it be a coincidence? Of course, there was still the tiniest chance that Heaven was the coincidence, that it really was Tasha that was the only intended victim. It could be that the killer just dumped that bottle in the first place he or she found when they were escaping down the alley. Maybe the car, the note, the death, the husband, the beautiful victim, maybe it was all purely chance. But chance or not, Heaven was in a tight spot. She couldn't wait for time to sort things out.

Heaven resurfaced. The scared, lost kid inside her had driven the van into downtown Kansas City. With surprise Heaven realized she was easing into a parking space very near the law office of Sandy Martin on Twelfth and Grand. This must mean something, Heaven thought. She locked the back doors of the van and slipped an hour's worth of change in the meter. It must mean it's lawyer time again. God forbid.

Beside the fact that she was one, even if not in good standing, Heaven always had an ever-changing need for various types of attorneys.

First, there were the real estate experts whom she had learned to call on for lease negotiations and the like. Her friend Sally Poronto did that.

Sally had really come through for Heaven when they had worked on the Cafe Heaven lease. It was Sally who suggested asking for such a long time frame, a ten-year lease with another ten-year option. Her theory was that the area would probably keep improving, if ever so slightly, and every time they had to go back to the negotiating table it would cost more rent money. Sally also pointed out that it made the business more saleable, should Heaven ever decide to move to Maine.

"Not that anyone would want the crazy place," Heaven mumbled to herself as she approached a tall building housing a bank and lawyers of all styles. She entered the lobby and made for the elevator, absentmindedly pressing the Up button.

Heaven glanced at the building directory. There were the tax attorneys, divorce lawyers, probate experts, deal makers. Heaven had used all the specialties at one time or the other. And, of course, there were the criminal lawyers. She'd needed one of those a time or two. Knowing who was hot right now, who was on the good side of the cops, who had been on a winning streak with juries, that was information only a practicing attorney had. She needed Sandy for that.

As the elevator door opened and she stepped on, a nasal voice yelled out, "Heaven, hold the door, gal." It was Cindy O'Brien, Sandy's secretary. She crammed herself in the last remaining slot on the elevator car and punched the sixteenth floor button.

"H, what in the hell is going on?" Cindy was not going to waste time waiting for privacy.

"Your guess is as good as mine, Cindy. She just dropped dead in Sandy's arms."

"I've seen it happen before. After all, your ex *is* a lady-killer. But never before has it been quite this literal, if you know what I mean." Cindy was chewing Double Bubble as she talked.

"The cops were here this morning, going through Tasha's office with a fine-tooth comb. Now there's a Detective Stein up there, going through her Rolodex. What a charming person he isn't. Sandy is fit to be tied. Everyone in the office had the news on last night, or they saw the replay this morning."

From the looks on the faces of the other elevator occupants, everyone in Kansas City had been watching the news the night before. They were eagerly listening without looking at either Cindy or Heaven, everyone jumping off at his or her own floor to tell their coworkers they had just come up in the elevator with the Cafe Heaven woman, you know, the place where the pickets and the television cameras and the dead diner had converged. The sixteenth floor seemed hours away but finally they made it. Heaven and Cindy took a right turn to the firm of White, White, Klein and Martin.

A Robert Rauschenberg print hung on the wall behind the reception desk. Modern Italian leather chairs were poised and ready to accept rich bottoms. Yes, Heaven thought, Sandy has finally hit the big time. Good for him.

Sandy had evolved into a courtroom lawyer in the civil litigation trade. But it had taken twenty years of personal injury and divorce and small business representation to get him where he was now. Five years ago, White, White and Klein, one of the premier small firms in Kansas City had offered him a full partnership.

He was their litigation specialist, and business was so good that he had three young lawyers doing research for him. Tasha had been hired to be his samurai second.

"Come around with me, H. You might want to avoid that hallway." Cindy pointed left as she hustled Heaven right. They hadn't gone two steps when loud voices erupted from the left hallway and Tasha's office. As Cindy and Heaven turned toward the noise, they saw Harry Stein jerking on the collar of another man, an elegant, well-dressed man. Jason Kelley. The detective was pulling Jason out of the victim's office. Heaven turned toward Cindy for confirmation her eyes were not playing tricks.

"I'll just tell Sandy you're here." Cindy shook her head in disbelief.

At that moment Sandy Martin came out of the firm's law library.

"Katy, what are you doing here?"

"Never mind that now, what's he doing here?" Heaven pointed down the hallway at Detective Stein and Jason. She moved in their direction.

Sandy started toward them and stared. "What the hell, Stein?"

Harry Stein glared back angrily. "I take a half hour for lunch, and guess what I find when I get back to Tasha's office. Lover boy here, retrieving some letters from the quote, total stranger's, unquote, office. You didn't mention you were a pen pal of our victim earlier, lover boy. The same victim poisoned with the nicotine found in your car. Real twist of fate, eh?" Harry Stein held a wad of papers in the hand that wasn't around Jason's neck.

From this distance it did look like Jason's handwriting, Heaven thought, and made a lunge for Harry. She grabbed a couple of sheets of brown, natural looking paper. It was Jason's handwriting all right. She turned to him with the evidence in her hot little hand.

Heaven pushed on Jason's chest with her pointer finger. "You dog, what are you doing here? And you had the nerve to make me feel guilty about being jealous an hour ago? Do you actually know this woman?"

"Hey, that's evidence. Give that back." Harry was gesturing at Heaven.

"I can explain, Heaven, Detective. I know it looks bad." Jason's composure had finally cracked. The slicked back hair had come loose and was dangling over one eye. He was visibly shaking.

Sandy jumped into the fray. "Kelley, what the fuck is going on? Tasha never mentioned that you two had met. When . . . ? And what did Stein mean nicotine found in your car?"

Everyone started talking at once. Sandy Martin was making his hands into fists and yelling at Jason, how could he have known Tasha, what were they to each other, what did Jason do, just follow Sandy from woman to woman? Cindy was pulling on Sandy's jacket, trying to keep him away from Jason. At the same time she was yelling at Jason, asking how in the devil he had just sashayed into the office like that. Jason was actually clinging to Harry Stein for protection. At the same time he was yelling at Heaven, how he would have told her if she hadn't had to go off to that catering, how just like always, work interfered in their lives. Heaven was reading the letters out loud with a mixture of disbelief and sarcasm in her voice, had just gotten through the Hello Sweet Tasha greeting, when Harry Stein yelled, Whoa, and took out his handcuffs.

"Shut up, allaya. Now Jason and me have to have a little talk. The rest of you are going to have to wait until we're through. And the first person who says a word gets cuffed and I'll call a paddy wagon to take you three blocks to the station. Got it?"

Cindy, Sandy and Heaven stopped in their tracks. Harry retrieved the letters from Heaven, grabbed Jason by the arm and said, "We're going over to my office, where it's not so fucking insane. You people are crazy. I'm sealing the victims' office. If anyone goes in there you'll never practice law again, Martin. I mean it." Harry seemed to be positively enjoying himself.

Cindy O'Brien turned toward the reception area where several members of the staff were gathering in a little clump, murmuring and glancing from Harry and Jason to Sandy and Heaven nervously. Cindy strode off toward the sightseers.

"Don't tell me two of the men in my life were also two of the men in Tasha's life. Don't tell me that."

Heaven looked at Sandy. What she really wanted to say was, have you been fucking her?

"Now, let's not jump to conclusions, H. Calm down. I should calm down too."

Heaven didn't have a pithy crack left in her. "Sandy, I'm a mess. I need help."

"We all do, Katy." Sandy led her into his office, a black leather, Oriental rug affair with a great Wayne Thiebaud painting on the wall. It was of food, of course. Lemon pie.

"Nice painting, Sandy."

"Yeah, I traded it for a divorce. That was back in the days when I didn't have so much overhead and I could waste my billable hours on divorce work. Heaven, tell me everything that happened this morning. What did Tasha die of?"

"First, you have to tell me the truth. Were you and Tasha doing it?"

"I want to tell you it's none of your business, but I guess under the circumstances I can't. I met Tasha about ten months ago at a Bar Association meeting in New Orleans. You know how New Orleans is, you go to Bourbon Street, you go hear music, you dance, the next thing you know you're in love for a night. That was Tasha and me. She let me know right away she was living with someone, and I was dating someone more or less full time. Well, we kept in touch, you know, called once in a while. When the firm said I could hire someone with more courtroom experience I mentioned it to Tasha and she said she was ready for a change. She came for an interview and everyone here thought she was the one. But I felt uncomfortable because of, you know, New Orleans. We talked about it and agreed that if she came to Kansas City, our relationship would be only business. And we had stuck to that. Except for some harmless flirting and I guess, some flirting a little more serious, like last night."

"So you probably would have gone to bed with her last night, but doggone the luck, she up and died instead." Heaven was pacing, thinking about Jason and what his story would be. "Did she ever mention Jason to you?"

"I don't exactly remember. Of course, you came up. Tasha had wanted to go to your place last night. She was real curious, and I think she wanted to see you. I guess I thought it was because of me. What a kick in the old ego if she was just trying to make Jason jealous."

"Maybe she had a bad feeling about the evening and insisted you come to the cafe so she could ruin my life by being murdered there."

"Katy, get a grip. You don't have time for self-pity. You need to at least think about a criminal lawyer. And you need to tell me everything I missed this morning."

"What about that woman that defends death row prisoners?" Heaven knew she was being a tad too dramatic but Sandy had already ruled out self-pity.

"Okay, Okay, Katy, calm down. Let's make a few calls." Sandy closed the office door to a number of curious stares.

Chapter 9

Detective Bonnie Weber gazed idly out of her window at police headquarters. Its location at Twelfth and Locust was situated right next to City Hall, Jackson County Courthouse and Municipal Court. You could always see some interesting deal being made on the streets below.

Bonnie saw a defense lawyer and a prosecutor locked in conversation in front of Municipal Court. Two cops and an aide to the mayor crossed the street, laughing together. A judge and a city councilwoman sidled into the Lincoln Inn for lunch. She turned back to the room and her victim. Harry Stein had to testify in court at the two o'clock session, so he had told Bonnie what had happened and left Jason with her.

"You and Heaven were married how long?"

"From 1988 until about six months ago. November, I guess it was. But I moved out last June."

"So what happened?"

"The restaurant happened. We stopped having a life together. I got tired of going to bed alone."

"So you wanted the split, not her?"

"She hadn't even noticed that we weren't on the same planet anymore."

"Right. I guess you got her attention, eh?"

"When I moved out, yes, she noticed."

"Angry?"

"And hurt. She couldn't understand what the big fuss was about. She was just going along with her life like always. Heaven expects those close to her to be prepared for whatever she is doing that year."

"So you were the angry one, Jason buddy?"

"Yes, Detective, I was pissed off. I thought I'd found someone to spend my life with, and she evaporated in a cloud of kitchen smoke."

"Right. Let's see if I've got last night right, Jason, old buddy. You went to the restaurant around six yesterday evening to trade cars with Heaven. She asked you to move the car around back so it wouldn't get stolen or pissed in. That's where the note, *"Your wish is my command"* comes in. Then you took her van home, moved whatever, and were in a meeting with your client until eleven. You brought the van back when we all had our A.M. powwow at the cafe. You get ready to leave in your car and the bottle and note came floating out of nowhere."

"You were there, Detective, you were there."

"And I have the names of your clients who are opening a brew pub out in the suburbs. Before I call them, you sure you're covered?"

"Positive. I went home to get a large poster, an antique beer poster that I wanted to use in the pub. It was already framed so I couldn't fit it in my car. I took it and met these two brothers, the Winston brothers, on One hundred nineteenth and Roe, in Johnson County. We spent the rest of the evening going over the kitchen plans. The equipment company was delivering the exhaust system today and we wanted to be sure we had everything in the right place. Once you install the exhaust you don't have the luxury of moving stoves and ovens around."

"Right. I'll want to talk to the Winston brothers today so you might want to let them know. Employers always get nervous when the police call. Now let's go over Tasha again. You met her at the Nelson Gallery, at some swanky opening I bet."

"At the restaurant in Rozelle Court, actually. She was by herself reading and having a glass of wine, and I was meeting someone who was late. We started talking and I asked her to go to the Grand Emporium the next night to see Robert Cray. I think it was the end of March or maybe the beginning of April."

"And you've been seeing her since then?"

"Not every night. Not hot and heavy but yes, we have been together quite a bit."

Bonnie tossed one of the notes across the desk to Jason. He picked it up and then quickly put it back down, blushing. "You don't call this hot and heavy, Jason? Well, buddy, I'd like to know what you consider hot and heavy then. When did you find out Tasha was working with Sandy Martin?"

"It must have been the third or fourth time we went out. It was time for the what-brought-you-to-Kansas City-when-you-had-such-an-exciting-job-in-the-Big Apple conversation. Before that we had just talked about her being an attorney and her work in New York and what books she liked and art and music and stuff. Date stuff. But then we went to bed and entered the next phase, I guess."

"And when she said who she worked with, did you spill the beans?"

"Not then. I was shocked. It's such a damn small town. I guess I had to think. How would Sandy react to my dating a lawyer in his office? It's not like Sandy and I have bad blood. After all, Heaven had several relationships in between us. But I had stepped on his turf, and Tasha did tell me she had slept with him at a convention. I guess I just wanted to think it over."

"So when didja?"

"When did I tell her that I had been married to the same woman her boss had been married to? About two weeks ago. We'd been seeing each other a month or so, and I knew I wanted to continue seeing her. Because it's such a damn small town I thought I should come clean. I could just see us enjoying ourselves somewhere and Sandy showing up. 'What in the hell are you two doing together?'—that sort of thing. Besides, I had nothing to hide. I wasn't married anymore."

"What was the deceased's reaction?"

"Detective, you did that on purpose didn't you, calling Tasha deceased? I still can't believe . . ." Jason paused and looked like he would burst into tears. "She was totally amazed. It is a little far-fetched if you don't know how this town operates."

"Right. What else? Pissed, jealous?"

"She asked a million questions about Heaven. I guess it created a bond between them, even if Heaven didn't know about it."

"Are you sure Heaven didn't know?"

"What are you driving at, Detective? That Heaven was following me around and found out who I was seeing and put two and two together and started plotting to poison her? Oh, come on. Why would she do such a stupid thing? In her own place? She didn't want me anymore anyway. It doesn't make sense."

"Who says she doesn't want you? You wanted out, not her. When a marriage goes bad it leads people to do crazy things, Jason buddy. It led you to walk out the door, now didn't it?"

"Yes, it did. Did it lead me to pick up a beautiful stranger in the restaurant of the Nelson Gallery, yes. Did I choose someone who I thought Heaven might really be pissed off by? I guess, unconsciously, but I didn't have a clue she worked for Sandy when I started seeing her. I didn't loiter outside Sandy Martin's law office to pick up his female employees just to piss Heaven off. And I don't think for a minute Heaven would be mad enough or jealous enough to harm anyone. Was I mad enough to hatch a diabolical plot to frame her for murder? Did I murder an innocent person to make her look bad? Will I not be happy until Cafe Heaven is shuttered and padlocked? No way. I stupidly wanted my wife to open a restaurant as much as she wanted to open one. I have had clients who own restaurants and still have a family life. I thought we could be like them but it wasn't to be. It's my fault as much as it is her fault. I still care about her. The restaurant won, I lost. We go on about our lives. I hope."

"Right." Bonnie swiveled her desk chair toward the window again. "I hope you're right, Jason buddy. But one person doesn't get to go on with their life. So neither does the killer if I have anything to do with it."

Bonnie got up and went around the desk to stand in front of Jason Kelley.

"Thanks for helping to clarify this ugly little mess. You know the routine. If you think of something, find another note in the old MG, get a threatening phone call, you tell me first. And, Kelley, do bring me that other letter you mentioned, the one you got from Tasha thanking you for, whatever. We need to eliminate the notion that you might have been involved with Tasha for a lot longer than you're willing to admit. It does have a date on it, I hope?"

"I wish I could remember, Detective. Dates are the last thing you think about when you get a note from a beautiful woman. But you will have it in your hands this afternoon, I promise. I have to do some work but I'll send it over by messenger. Good luck. Keep Heaven out of jail. Keep me out of jail." The door slammed behind him.

Bonnie Weber sat silently. That poor jerk Jason was in a mess of trouble. Even if everything he said checked out, and all these little coincidences were just that, he had lost his girlfriend and his ex-wife was in danger. From something or someone. Finally Bonnie stopped staring out the window and stood up for a stretch. She had missed her run this morning, unable to move when the alarm went off three hours after she had gone to bed.

"Now it's just you and me, asshole." Bonnie always talked to the elusive perpetrators. It made them more real, less slippery, and she could yell at them.

Time for the lists.

Bonnie got out a stack of virgin legal pads. On the first pad she wrote VICTIM. Under that heading she spent about fifteen minutes writing down all the chores she needed to attend to. Parents, ex-coworkers, present coworkers, ex-lovers or husbands all had to be located. Tasha had to be reconstructed on paper. On the next legal pad she wrote SUSPECTS. First on this list she wrote Heaven Lee. Below Heaven's name she scrawled:

> seen arguing with victim thirty minutes before death—
> had access to food and drink—
> empty bottle of nicotine found in the car she was driving.

Next she listed Sandy Martin:

> with the victim all the time leading up to her death—
> romantic involvement—
> had access to food and drink.

Then Jason Kelley:

> wrote incriminating note—
> bottle of nicotine in his car—
> alibi but could have accomplice.
> romantic involvement with both the victim and Heaven—
> was victim blackmailing him?
> would Sandy or Heaven care?

Then Fudge Patrol:

> were at the scene—
> had access to food and drink—
> moral belief in cause can create lots of shit—

do any of the patrol know Heaven personally, know Tasha?

Bonnie paused and then wrote:

was target Tasha?
was target Heaven, personal or business?
was target restaurant?
was target restaurant employees?
was it a complete nut, Tylenol killer style

She hoped by the end of the day she would have more names on this pad. She was hoping for some juicy leads to fall onto the page.

The next legal pad became the PHYSICAL EVIDENCE pad. Here Bonnie would translate the medical examiner's jargon into her own words.

On the next pad Bonnie wrote MOTIVE. She stared at that pad a long time. She didn't have much. Nothing that made sense as a motive for murder. But Bonnie had learned a long time ago that sense and murder don't go together. A kid standing on the street gets shot so someone can join a gang. A neighbor's dog barks too loud. The neighbor gets shot. Motives usually look pretty weak on paper. She made her initial list.

Heaven: Jealous of Sandy Martin. Tasha insulted her about her disbarment. Found out Jason was seeing Tasha, jealous.

Sandy: Lover spurned? Found out Tasha was seeing Jason. Office problems. Revenge on Heaven.

Jason: Revenge on Heaven. Lover spurned? Blackmail, to keep Tasha quiet, because Tasha would tell

Heaven they were seeing each other before the divorce. Were they seeing each other before the divorce?

What a mess, Bonnie thought. The only thing she could hope for was an easy answer from Tasha and her past.

Bonnie picked up the phone and started to work.

It was close to seven o'clock when Evidence Technician Scotty Sutter stuck his head in the detective's office.

"Bonnie, it's been so quiet in here everybody thought you were napping."

"No, Scotty, I've been standing on my fucking head, meditating. Whaddya got?"

"No prints on the bottle. Not even a good smudge. Looks like someone used gloves. The paper has some so-so prints but they belonged to the guy you had me print this afternoon, Jason Kelley. That help?"

"I'm not surprised. Thanks, Scotty."

"Go home, Bonnie." Scotty bowed out.

Maybe it was time for a look at the legal pads. It was hard to work the phones at this hour. Dinnertime in New York. Businesses were closed, even in Kansas City. Bonnie pulled the VICTIM pad to the top of the pile.

Tasha Arnold was actually Tasha Aronowitz. She had shortened her name when she was accepted at the Dalton School, that bastion of WASP-dom in New York City. The name change had been her parents idea.

Through Sandy Martin, Bonnie had obtained the phone numbers and other pertinent data about Tasha's folks. Although Sandy had called them the night before with the tragic news, Bonnie had the unpleasant task of telling them the autopsy findings, trying to be respectful and ask questions at the same time.

Both of Tasha's parents were attorneys. They lived in Manhattan, Upper West Side, in the Eighties, on Broadway. They thought Tasha had lost her mind three months ago when she said she was leaving for the midwest. Now that she'd up and been poisoned they were sure she'd gone nuts. Yes, the father was flying out this evening to bring the body home, when will it be released? No, their daughter had no enemies that they were aware of. Yes, she had been married once, in law school. The ex-husband currently lived in Italy. No, of course she had no children. No, she had not dealt with dangerous criminals, only white-collar crime. But maybe the detective should talk to Tasha's associates at the U.S. Attorneys' office.

The federal district attorney, Tasha's old boss, was shocked. He thought Tasha was crazy three months ago when she said she was leaving to move to the midwest. This just proved he was right. Yes, Tasha had been one of their prime courtroom stars. No, not drug dealers, not Colombian maniacs. She had dealt with civilized white-collar criminals. Junk bond traders, bank embezzlers, insider trading scandals, that had been Tasha's forte. Most of these guys paid huge fines, did a split six, still had millions in Grand Cayman in the bank. Nothing personal. No nasty scenes. No one had committed suicide that he recalled. No vengeful relatives who thought Tasha had ruined their life. Yes, Tasha had been seeing someone, another attorney in the office. No, they had stopped dating six months ago. No, no hard feelings that he could see. But maybe the detective should talk to the man herself.

Stanley Hiller was appalled. He thought Tasha had taken leave of her senses to leave the U.S. Attorneys' office, for Christ sakes, to move to Kansas City? Yes, he and Tasha had been lovers for about two years. No, nothing had gone wrong. It was just that he had an ex-wife and two young daughters and, well, they had decided to give it another try. Yes, I guess you could say he left his wife for Tasha. No, why would his wife still resent her? They were happily back together. Yes, as a matter of fact, she *had* been rather relieved that Tasha had moved out of town. No, Tasha had understood. Yes, Tasha had had a roommate before they moved in together. A woman in the rag trade. Yes, he thought he did have that number.

And so it had gone. After hours of this, Bonnie felt reasonably sure no one from Tasha's past had flown to Kansas City, snuck into Cafe Heaven where she happened to be dining, poisoned her wine or risotto, tossed the empty poison bottle in the vintage car parked in the back alley. They didn't even seem to know where Kansas City was.

Tomorrow she'd go over the stuff Harry Stein had found at the Kansas City law office and Tasha's Crown Center apartment. Then she would pay a little visit to Jason Kelley. He had sent the note from Tasha over to her. It was dated 4-5. It was a sweet and clever note, saying how glad she was that she had met Jason, that she hoped they would have many more nights like the night before.

Bonnie had also talked to Jason's clients, the guys who were opening the brew pub. They were sorry about the mess that Jason was in, and yes, they had been with Jason that night. When it came to the time frame, they weren't sure what time Jason had arrived.

They wanted to help, but they hadn't paid any attention to the time. Yes, Bonnie would have to shake Jason's tree a little more. But not until tomorrow.

Bonnie picked up the pad marked PHYSICAL EVIDENCE. Quickly she added the info Scotty had given her about the bottle and the note. The rest of the page was filled with information about nicotine. Amazing how lethal it was.

The doc seemed to know a lot about it. He told her about a guy whose wife replaced his aftershave with nicotine sulfate, he slathered it on and was dead in twenty minutes. Goes right in through the skin. Or you can ingest it like Tasha did. Kills quick, the doc said. Death occurs between five minutes and four hours after contact which meant to Bonnie that Tasha could have been doused even before she got to Cafe Heaven. But probably not. Doc said this stuff first stimulates the brain, then paralyzes it. The whole nervous system, brain, spinal cord, skeletal structure, muscles, all stop. And, of course, the respiratory system. It stops too. Death usually results from respiratory failure due to paralysis of the muscles. Convulsions, coma, death. And the stuff also kills bugs.

Bonnie had called some nurseries and garden supply centers and asked about nicotine sulfate. Although they didn't carry it anymore they all said the hard-core rose gardners all still used it. Cost about five bucks a bottle. They said that gardeners who couldn't get their hands on the bottled product would go up to Weston, Missouri, to the tobacco sale barn. For a few dollars they could buy some tobacco, boil it up and have a fine substitute.

A lot cheaper than the Uzis the kids like to shoot each other with, Bonnie thought.

The PHYSICAL EVIDENCE pad was tossed in a pile with the other scribbled pads. Nothing would change on them tonight.

Detective Bonnie Weber called her husband, made a deal to bring home Chinese if he'd put a bottle of wine on ice, grabbed her jacket and hit the road.

Chapter 10

Angel Rodriquez pushed his chair back from the desk. He felt exhausted and elated all at the same time. It had been a busy day. Since his visit with his partners the night before he had three new properties almost sewed up and ready to sign.

A farmer in Holden, Missouri, who had inherited two houses on Genessee Street agreed to sell them to Angel. Too much trouble driving in to take care of them, he said. Too hard to get good renters. Taxes ate up everything you made.

More importantly, Angel had finally struck a deal with the owner of the biker bar, Clyde Bugg. Clyde had bought the property in 1979 and was ready to turn a good profit and move to Arkansas. The neighborhood was going downhill, he said. Too many yuppies. Too many arty types. Why, he couldn't remember the last time there had been a good brawl in the place, couldn't remember the last time he had broken a pool cue over someone's head. He'd take Angel's money and run with it, happy to leave Thirty-ninth Street to Angel and the yuppies and fags. They were too dull.

Then there was the unexpected crisis across the street at Cafe Heaven. What a break this could be for Angel.

Cafe Heaven had, by far, the longest lease of anyone on that side of the street. Angel knew Heaven had already been approached by her landlord about what would happen if he, the landlord, sold the building. Heaven had pointed to the paragraph in the lease that said she would have to be adequately compensated if a new owner terminated the lease before it was up.

That meant seventeen years of compensation to Heaven and an expensive problem to Angel's partners.

The current owner pointed out to Angel that he had a long-term tenant and that made the building more valuable, didn't it? To Angel the long-term lease was a liability, not a plus. Nobody wants a long-term tenant for a building that you have plans to tear down. But he couldn't say that to the building's owner. No one could know quite yet what was going to happen on Thirty-ninth Street.

The Cafe Heaven lease had been a real pain in the ass for Angel. Until now. If Heaven was in jail she couldn't very well run a restaurant, could she? Even just the fact that someone had died there couldn't be good for business. It had been on TV for Christ's sake. He couldn't have planned it better.

Angel shifted in his chair. He had an uneasy feeling. It had started this morning when he had heard the news. It was almost too perfect. Fate? Or something else?

Someone had murdered that woman, that part was clear after the medical examiner released his report today. Angel had heard that part on the radio. It was probably someone from her past. After all, she was a lawyer from New York. But Sal said that she and Heaven had words just a few minutes before she collapsed. That was probably just a coincidence, like her dying in front of Heaven's place. It was a coincidence he hoped to use to his advantage.

But the uneasy feeling in the back of his mind told him his associates were not above putting Heaven Lee in a bad situation. Of course, none of them, Angel included, were anywhere near Thirty-ninth Street when the incident occurred. They were at a steak house downtown. Alibis for everyone. But the uneasy feeling didn't go away just because Angel knew where his partners had been last night. After all, if they liked doing things themselves they wouldn't need Angel, now would they?

Angel had a new timetable. He had until the end of June to get this block wrapped up. That gave him less than two months.

Tomorrow would be a good day to go across the street and pay Heaven Lee a visit. While she was still scared. Before they found the real killer.

Angel didn't think for a minute the real killer was Heaven. They were hardly bosom buddies, but he liked her spunk and thought she was a hard worker. He wished she didn't think he was scum.

But Heaven and he both did what it took to survive. And tonight, for Angel, that meant going west down Thirty-ninth Street to pay a visit to the Kountry Kraft shop two doors down from the strip joint. He heard their business was bad. He heard the knitters and the needlepoint fans didn't like to walk past the strip joint to buy their supplies. Maybe Angel could make a deal.

Chapter 11

It was now Wednesday morning. Angel Rodriquez trudged up the alley to the back door of Cafe Heaven. Good smells and laughter greeted him. It made his stomach ache because he knew the laughter would stop as soon as the Heaven crew saw him. Buying up Thirty-ninth Street had not exactly made him popular with his neighbors, especially since last year when he leased the old Diamond Theater to the Spelling brothers for their strip joint juice bar.

Thirty-ninth Street had a very active neighborhood association, and they hated the idea of a strip joint. Neighborhood associations had considerable clout with the Liquor Control Board downtown. The board listened when the neighborhood committees came down and asked for no more liquor licenses to be issued in a particular neighborhood in Kansas City. They took the neighborhood recommendations into account when someone new applied for an existing slot. The Diamond would never stand a chance to be approved by the neighborhood or the city.

But the Spelling brothers got around that by not

asking for a liquor license. They charged four dollars for orange juice and laughed all the way to the bank. Since the women who took their clothes off at the Diamond couldn't be accused of trying to get poor, innocent gentlemen drunk, they could sit down at the table and . . . visit.

The whole scheme infuriated the older families and the new yuppies alike. They demanded a hearing at City Hall. The city shrugged and said that there was no basis for not issuing a retail business license. Angel shrugged and told the neighborhood association there was nothing he could do. He had been lucky to find any tenant for that big old place he said.

Everyone was furious at Angel and most churches had preached against him at least once. City councilmen were called. Letters to the editor of the *Kansas City Star* were written and duely printed in the paper.

The Thirty-ninth Street League of Decency was founded and started their fudge vigils outside the Diamond. They also appeared occasionally outside Angel's office.

As he opened the kitchen door of Cafe Heaven, the easy kitchen camaraderie turned into an uneasy silence. Heaven came in the door from the bar with both hands clutching bottles of wine. Brian and Pauline looked from Angel to Heaven and back again.

"Heaven, I'm so sorry about the trouble the other night. I saw the television coverage the next day. If you don't watch out you're going to give the neighborhood a bad name," Angel said in a jocular tone.

"No, Rodriquez, that's your department," Heaven retorted. "What brings you across the street? A little gloating, I suppose."

"Actually, I came to offer my help. I thought you might need some."

"The only help I need right now, Mr. Rodriquez, is someone who can give me a couple of extra hours in the day. We have a wine dinner tonight, and we have a lot of work to do. So this is where you say sorry that I bothered you and quietly get lost. I hope." Heaven emphasized the point by turning her back on Angel and stirring a huge stockpot.

"Not so fast, lady, not so fast. Don't you at least want to hear what I have to say before you send me out the door?"

Angel knew the answer to that question, but it didn't stop him. He had an intimidation style that combined extreme courtesy with constant, steady pressure. It worked in the long run. He knew this wasn't going to be a piece of cake but it wasn't time to go back across the street with his tail between his legs either.

Heaven whirled around with a flash of anger in her eyes.

"Okay, let's get this over with. I should have guessed you'd be over here like a bad personal injury lawyer at the scene of an accident. Come with me, said the fly to the spider."

With that Heaven opened the door to the now empty dining room, and jerked Angel through the door by the sleeve of his steel gray double-breasted Italian suit. Angel glanced over at the waiters station.

"Aren't you even going to offer me a cup of coffee?" He knew this was getting on Heaven's nerves, the formality, the civility of it all.

"Listen to me, buster. I don't have the time or temperament for this today. But you've insisted so here we are. Don't fuck with me another second. Spit it out or I'll walk away right now. What do you want, as if I didn't know?"

"As I said, Heaven, I just want to help. If, God forbid, this unfortunate death leads to a situation in which you can't continue to run the restaurant, I want you to know I can relieve you of the pressure of that long lease you have. I have two or three people that have contacted me about putting something on Thirty-ninth Street and as you know, the city won't issue any more liquor licenses here. The neighborhood association, in its misguided zeal, has vowed to oppose any more licenses and the city agreed to go along with this antiquated stance. So this space, that already has a liquor license, could be put right to use, if, you know, you can't, if you aren't able, for whatever reason. Or if business suffers too much from such unappetizing publicity, you may want out. And I'm there for you if that should occur. That's all I wanted to say." Angel gave a courtly little bow at the end of his speech, and then smiled a full court press smile.

Even Heaven felt the heat of that smile.

"Very funny, Rodriquez, but this isn't your lucky day. Oh, I want out all right. Every time someone doesn't show up or something breaks or I get another tax bill in the mail, I want to get in the van and drive to Bali in the worst way. And when customers fall dead outside the joint in front of TV cameras, going to Bali doesn't seem far enough.

"But give up this space to you? I don't think so. You and your clients, whoever they are, will not get this property without a good fight until well into the next millennium. Even if I'm thrown in jail I'll make damn sure that you can't get your hands on this corner because you've sold your own neighborhood down the river for a buck.

"You're low and this conversation is over." Heaven returned the courtly bow and held the door to the kitchen open for Angel.

"But of course, you have work to do," Angel said, pausing in the doorway. "A wine dinner did you say? How lucky that you still have support in this city."

He smiled. "But you've been in hot water before. You have weathered bad publicity before. Some would say you are an expert at it, wouldn't they? I hope that this turns out to be just a small inconvenience, and you are cleared of any wrongdoing very soon. In the meantime, my offer of help remains."

Angel moved quickly through the kitchen and out the back door. He didn't want to give Heaven a chance for another volley. The first set had gone as he expected it to go.

She's a worthy adversary, Angel thought, not like that rube farmer from Holden. For just a moment, Angel Rodriquez loved his job.

Chapter 12

Even though Heaven wanted to stop and pout over Angel's visit, she just didn't have the time. She didn't have time to call any of the lawyers Sandy had recommended. She didn't have time to worry anymore about Jason either. She had tried to find time to call him all evening yesterday but the cafe had been packed with every voyeur possible. She had almost forgotten about Tasha and the murder and Sandy and . . . What the hell was Jason writing to Tasha about? It sure had looked like Jason and Tasha were lovers from the letter she had briefly had her hands on. Reluctantly she filed that thought and all the questions that went with it.

There was a show to put on, after all. Even with the night crew coming in early they would all have their hands full. The theme of the food tonight was "Hidden Surprises." Every course was stuffed of filled or had one thing inside of another.

This meant more prep work, of course, but Heaven wanted the food to be more than special. She wanted it to be spectacular.

Every year Rowland Alexander left his Hunter Valley vineyard in Australia and came to America for a whirlwind two-week tour to promote the wines of Australia and his own Hunter Valley Winery, specifically. This used to be a hard task, back in the eighties before wine drinkers "discovered" Australian wines. Even three years ago, Rowland had had a difficult time getting one of the star chefs in Kansas City interested in pairing Aussie wines with their creations.

He came to Heaven as a second choice, and they both knew it. Heaven liked the wines and had quite a few of them on her list already. She and Rowland had hit it off, the first dinner had been a success, and now that Australian wines were very hot, Rowland had remained loyal to Heaven. Their dinners were always sold out as soon as they were announced. Tonight was no exception and there hadn't been a single cancellation because of the "incident." Heaven had called Rowland at his stop in New Orleans and explained the situation, but he had only laughed and said that he was in the United States for publicity, wasn't he?

It didn't hamper ticket sales to the wine crowd that Rowland Alexander was six-foot-four and drop-dead handsome, blessed with a distinguished gray beard and Paul Newman blue eyes. He was also a witty speaker and kept the crowd in the palm of his hand from the first course to the last.

Heaven could hardly wait for the bright spot in this dismal week. She buckled down.

The next thing she knew it was six-thirty and the staff was all assembled. There was a sign on the door explaining the cafe was closed for a private party tonight.

Pauline and the rest of the day crew went home but Brian stayed to help plate the courses. The lamb was due to go in the oven in an hour or so. Heaven went out and explained the concept and theme for the evening to the staff.

Rowland and the Australian Wine Council had decided they wanted to show how Australian wines went with many types of food so Rowland had requested an international menu. The idea of having hidden surprises was Heaven's. After going through the courses and the wines with Heaven, everyone in the front of the house settled in, polishing glasses and silverware. Guests were arriving for Yalumba, an Aussie sparkling wine at seven.

Heaven returned to the kitchen and the next thing she knew they were plating the first course, an international sampler of an oriental beggar's purse filled with mascarpone cheese spiked with wasabi mustard and pickled ginger, a Russian pirogi filled with caramelized red cabbage and a South American empanada full of spicy pumpkin and raisins. All these filled pastries were served with a Semillion from Southern Australia.

Three Fillings for Won Ton Wrappers
Ginger Cheese

   1 lb. mascarpone cheese, if mascarpone is unavailable, use a well-mixed combination of $^2/_3$ cream cheese, $^1/_3$ ricotta cheese

   2-4 T. wasabi mustard paste, to taste

   $^1/_3$ cup pickled ginger, chopped

   1 bunch green onions, sliced skinny

Combine and let the mixture marry for at least an hour.

Russian Cabbage

2 yellow onions, preferably Vidalia if in season
1 large head red cabbage
2 T. unsalted butter
olive oil
1 T. kosher salt
2 T. sugar
1/4 cup wine vinegar

The main thing to remember about caramelizing onions and cabbage is to take your time. Time is the most important ingredient in this dish. Peel, split, slice the onions. Finely dice the cabbage. Heat a combination of butter and olive oil and add the onions and cabbage. Slowly saute for about 20 minutes, until the onions start to be translucent. Add the salt and sugar.

Continue to cook slowly, stirring occasionally until the onions have turned a caramel brown. This should take about an hour. Remove from heat and add the vinegar.

Pumpkin Picadillo

1 med. can pumpkin
1/3 cup stuffed green olives, chopped
1/3 cup golden raisins
1/3 cup toasted walnuts, chopped

$^1/_4$ teas. each, kosher salt, cinnamon,
cayenne pepper, allspice

Combine all the above.

Next, with a creamy Marsanne, Heaven had the magnificent Russian creation, the Kulebiaka. The oblong pie, the outside formed of puff pastry or sour cream pastry, is traditionally filled with layers of the best fish a family could afford, in Russia it was probably sturgeon, but Heaven chose salmon, then added dilled rice and wild mushrooms. Each slice was topped with a light sauce made with the same wild mushrooms and dill, just for good measure.

The next wine was Rowland Alexander's prize winning Shiraz. Heaven gambled that one of her favorite Italian dishes would make a great match.

Each guest had their own small loaf of Tuscan bread that had been scooped out and filled with a chicken liver pate spiked with juniper berries. On top of the pate nestled a roasted quail stuffed with Italian sausage. Then the top of the bread was replaced. After the quail was eaten, the bread covered with pate was pulled apart and devoured. It was sort of an edible bowl and ten and twenty blackbirds baked in a pie, all rolled into one.

The crowd liked it so much, Heaven had to go out and accept cheers.

The Cabernet Sauvignon for the evening was a mammoth, ten-year-old monster. Heaven stuffed legs of lamb with Swiss chard, raisins, pine nuts and served thick, pink slices in a pool of sauce made from the same Cabernet.

Rowland told the history of each wine with his

usual wit and knowledge, throwing in lots of history of Australia in the bargain. Because of his charm and the good food, the front of the house was full of laughter, the tinkle of glasses, then the lull of sated appetites.

The back of the house was happy too, with the satisfaction of knowing they had done a good job. They were preparing a salad course of field greens, a melange of tiny lettuces like red oak and tango, radicchio and mizuna. These tender little shoots had been tossed with the lightest dressing of balsamic vinegar and good olive oil. As the crew plated this, Heaven took time for some ice water and a deep breath. But the feeling of well-being that had grown throughout the evening suddenly drained from her body.

The mix of greens, grown by a local organic farmer, didn't look the way it usually did. There was a dark green leaf that Heaven hadn't seen before. That is, she hadn't seen it since her childhood in Kansas. Heaven grabbed the huge bowl that Sara had tossed the greens in. She fished around until she had three or four of the deep green velvety specimens. They looked like Swiss chard but Heaven knew they weren't.

"Oh, God, no. Sara, have any of the greens gone out yet?" Heaven's voice had an edge of hysteria.

"No, I'm waiting till I get half of them plated," Sarah answered without turning around.

"Thank God. Throw them all back in the bowl. Everybody. Quick. We're changing this course. Get out that wheel of Stilton. Don't we have some pears? Give everyone a half of a pear sliced and a little chunk of Stilton. Hurry, hurry." Heaven's voice was shaking so, the whole kitchen was alarmed.

"What's the deal?" Sarah quickly started halving pears but she was also giving Heaven a look that said, Have you gone bonkers?

"There's rhubarb in the spring mix!" Heaven said this with the drama of a declaration of war crime guilt.

"So?" Brian asked. "Maybe Max is trying something new."

"Max wouldn't have tried something new with rhubarb. Rhubarb leaves are deadly poison. My grandfather used to grow rhubarb, and he would show it to me when I was little and tell me never to eat the leaves. Only the stems are good, and even they will make you have a stomach ache if you eat them raw. Poison, you guys. As in we could have killed ninety people in one fell swoop. Not one at a time like on Monday! At the very least we would have made them sick. Oh, God, I feel sick." Heaven bent over the counter, dizzy and confused, her head in her hands.

The whole kitchen was still for about ten seconds, then Sara took charge, barking orders that roused everyone from the evil spell.

"Okay, boss, we'll worry about that later. We have to get this course out the door and then, don't forget, we have a damn ice cream dessert. You just had to do ice cream for ninety. If it doesn't melt when we unmold those damn things we'll be lucky. Brian, take all that salad mess and put it back into the plastic bag. We'll examine that stuff later. Put it back in the walk-in. Now, guys, pears please, cheese please."

The show went on, thanks to Sara. Heaven was a wreck.

Dessert for the evening was an ice cream bombe. Heaven had lined the bombe molds with coffee ice cream. When that layer had hardened, it was lined with sponge cake. Then, there was the fudge sauce, then back in the freezer, then crunchy toffee, then vanilla ice cream studded with bits of amaretti cookies and toasted almonds. When it was cut it resembled a geological crosscut, an edible geode. Sliced and drizzled with fudge and caramel sauce, it made a fitting end to a meal that the crowd said was one of the best ever. Rowland's Late Harvest Riesling sent everyone over the top.

Heaven moved as if in a dream. She went out and sat down next to Rowland for dessert. She accepted the good wishes of the crowd. She conferred with Sam and Joe and Murray. She made sure everyone had paid. She watched as the guests left, she even had a cognac with Rowland, tried to flirt. When he left she made her way to the kitchen as the crew finished cleaning up.

"Brian, think hard. Were the greens here when you got in this morning? Did you see Max deliver the stuff? Help, help, help!"

"Calm down, boss, I remember for a change. Pauline and I both got here around seven-thirty and all the produce from the organic guy was stacked by the back door. The stuff from the regular produce company came later, about ten. Pauline said he's a real early bird. The organic guy I mean."

"I'm glad to hear that," Heaven murmured as she clutched the bag of greens close to her. "Because me and the greens are going to be on his doorstep in just a few hours."

"Do you think someone knew the theme of the dinner?" Sara wondered out loud. "Hidden surprises. In this case, hidden rhubarb leaves."

"Hidden surprises all right. Like hidden death. Surely no one is that sick. This must be a mistake. Max got his greens confused." Heaven tossed the bag back into the walk-in.

Everyone knew it was wishful thinking.

Chapter 13

Heaven Lee sat drinking coffee at the kitchen table of Max Mossman. It was eight the morning after. On the other side of the table sat Max and between them was the mound of soggy, wilted greens right where Heaven had dumped them in a temper tantrum earlier. Max was reading from a guide to common poisonous plants.

"It says that in England during World War One there was a food shortage and some dummy in the government said not to waste the leaves of the rhubarb plant. A bunch of people were poisoned."

"Great, Max. Mass death by rhubarb has already been done. What else?"

"Says the leaves have oxalic acid. This stuff, the oxalic acid, passes into the bloodstream and forms sharp crystals that plug up the kidneys."

"Ugh, that hurts just to hear about."

"Stomach pains, nausea, vomiting, difficulty of breathing, internal bleeding, coma and . . ." Max stopped his recitation.

"Death perhaps? Is that how that list ends, Max?"

Heaven's voice was full of anxiety. It was the voice of someone who hadn't slept much the night before. Heaven was very cranky.

Max put down the book. He got up and came around to Heaven's side of the lettuce pile, took her hand and pulled her to her feet.

"Come outside with me. You need to take a little walk around the grounds. You need to see for yourself there isn't a rhubarb plant on the place. I don't even have a patch for myself. I don't have any Swiss chard either. I don't plant chard until the fall. You'll see."

Heaven flipped through the pile of greens with her fingers. "But there it is, right between the mizuna and the frisee. You agree that it matches the picture, don't you?"

"Yes, yes, I agree that it's rhubarb. It just didn't come from here. It wasn't in that bag of greens when I dropped your order off. I'm as sure of that as I am of anything in the world, Heaven. My reputation is as much at stake as yours is. I do this for a living. I know what I grow and what I don't. I did make a big mistake, though."

"What now?" Heaven expected the worst.

"I should never have left that stuff outside your door unattended. I get up so early to pick the lettuces before they droop in the midday heat that I get to a lot of my accounts before the prep crew gets in. I also miss the commuter crowd if I leave early."

Max lived in the half-farm, half-suburban area of Louisburg, Kansas. He had a fifty-acre truck farm, but he was still only an hour away from the restaurants of Kansas City. Forty-five minutes away early in the morning.

"Who would think that some maniac would spike the spring mix with deadly greens." Heaven shook her head in dismay.

Max and Heaven went out the kitchen door to begin their inspection tour. It was a glorious spring day. Even Heaven felt better for a minute.

"Yeah, I think for now, until we figure out what's going on, I better see my orders into the walk-in. Not just at your place, everywhere. Until we know what we're up against. Could be some nut who hates vegetables." Max led Heaven out toward the strawberry beds.

After Heaven left the farm she stopped by the cafe to check for messages and further disasters. Everything was quiet for a change so she headed downtown to the police station. She had called Bonnie Weber from the farm and made an appointment. She wanted to be the one to tell her about the rhubarb. She sure didn't want Harry Stein to come snooping around and have Brian say something like, "Whoa, dude, we almost took out the whole dining room last night." Heaven was also scared to death. She wanted Bonnie to reassure her. Fat chance.

Bonnie Weber was irate. "Right. What a fuckin' fool. He just leaves his shit outside the door where anyone could spit on the asparagus, is that what you're tellin me?"

"Not anymore. But don't be mad at Max. He's scared too. Think of what this means, Bonnie. It must mean that whoever killed Tasha isn't done yet. Either they're throwing us off the track by the rhubarb thing, or someone has a gripe against me or . . . I don't know what. It couldn't be Tasha."

"Not so fast, not so fast. I do agree with you that

this new incident points toward you and away from Tasha's personal life, but the two incidents could be unrelated, Heaven. What if someone who has a hard-on for you or someone else at Cafe Heaven took this opportunity to twist the knife. They didn't have anything to do with Tasha, but they planted the poisonous plants hoping we'd think it was related to the first death. We still don't have enough to go down any one path yet. But, Heaven, I don't know how much longer I can let you stay open."

Heaven felt as though she'd been slapped.

"What are you talking about?"

"Do you want to put your customers at risk, Heaven?" Ninety people could have died or been sent to the hospital last night. What makes you think it won't happen again? Whether there's a copycat nut out there or the first killer is still at it, it makes no difference if someone else dies. If, and I mean if, we don't get a good solid lead in the next week, I'll feel compelled to close Cafe Heaven. Last resort. Do you understand me? Do you even hear me?"

Heaven's eyes had glazed over. She quickly snapped back to earth.

"You can't! What about all the people who depend on my place for their living?"

"Right. If someone else gets poisoned, all those people won't be making the rent anyway. You know that. If someone is still trying to poison your customers surely you don't want to wait till they succeed again, do you? No, I know you. I know that you'll see it my way. It's tough, Heaven. I'm sorry."

"I know, I know. I will never forgive myself if something else happens. But tell me the truth, do you see any light at the end of the tunnel? Do you have a suspect? Beside me, of course."

"I can't really discuss it."

"Well, Bonnie, thanks for the week. I guess I just have to find the killer before you have to close us down."

"Heaven, you did the right thing by telling me. I would have found out about the rhubarb, believe me. But you won't be doing the right thing if you stick your nose into police business."

"What choice do I have? I can't just twiddle my thumbs, for God's sake."

"Heaven, don't forget you're not an officer of the court anymore. Don't cross the line. Don't get in my face. Don't break the law and don't, don't fuck with Harry Stein. He doesn't trust you. I mean it!" Bonnie Weber was yelling at her friend.

"I promise I'll just try to figure out who might want to do this to me. There must be something that only I know. Or Murray knows. Or Sam. We'll just put our heads together, that's all."

"Right. Remember, it may not be you they're after. Heaven, butt out. I mean it."

"Bonnie, I mean it too," Heaven said as she walked out.

As soon as the door was closed, Detective Bonnie Weber picked up the phone. She still needed to find Jason Kelley and try to pin down his timetable Monday night.

Heaven didn't think of using the phone to find Jason. She drove straight to his apartment at the Sophian Plaza. The Sophian was a beautiful apartment building on the edge of the Country Club Plaza. It was the first stop for many a well-to-do Kansas City man or woman after a divorce. Jason had taken a two bedroom with a formal dining room, twenty-foot-high ceilings, a redone kitchen. Jason used the extra bedroom for an office. Heaven had visited for dinner once. It had been tense for both of them, and she had not been back. But this afternoon Heaven positively peeled up in front of the stuffy facade, or as much of a peel as a catering van can provide. Quickly she ran to the front door and rang. "Yes?" the familiar voice said.

"Let me in." She did not waste words and neither did he. The door buzzed open.

When Heaven reached the seventh floor, Jason was waiting outside his door in the hall. He was wearing an Armani shirt and pleated pants. He had on a pair of wire rimmed glasses and was carrying a drafting pencil.

"I knew you'd be around soon. I guess you want to know about Tasha."

"How'd you guess?" Heaven strode past Jason into the apartment.

An hour later, she and Jason were cuddled on the couch, a bottle of wine half drunk on the table in front of them. Heaven was crying.

"I'm a mess, and I'm scared, and I'm sorry I ruined our life, and I guess I believe you about Tasha. You always loved to send those corny love letters. They must work every time," Heaven said, halfheartedly punching Jason's arm.

Jason turned Heaven's face up toward his and kissed her, a long, lingering kiss. It was not a hey-kid-have-a-good-life kiss. It was an I-still-love-you kiss.

The doorbell rang. Jason and Heaven both jumped as if they had been caught by a *National Enquirer* photographer. Jason reluctantly let go of Heaven and went to the speaker phone. It was Detective Bonnie Weber. He buzzed her up.

"What does Bonnie want?" Heaven asked as she put on her shoes.

"I guess she wants to go over my alibi one more time." Jason shifted uncomfortably and glanced away from Heaven's gaze.

"You mean you're still a suspect too?" Heaven was ready to unleash a new round of crying. She stood up instead and tried to collect her thoughts and emotions. The kiss had brought back lots of memories, good and bad. Before the kiss, Jason had told her how he had met Tasha and how lonely he had been after they separated. Heaven had felt guilty one more time for the breakup of their marriage. Even though she knew in her heart she had not meant to spoil things, Jason always told her they would still be together if she had just not taken him for granted. Even the best relationships need tending, he had said.

The magic moment was over. Bonnie was on her way up, and Jason was acting like he still had something to hide, quickly removing the wine and glasses into the kitchen. Heaven left without saying goodbye. As she headed for the elevator, the doors opened and Bonnie Weber walked out.

"He's all yours," Heaven said glumly.

"Heaven," Bonnie yelled. "Butt out. I mean it."

Chapter 14

The sign in the window at Sal's said GONE TO LUNCH, BE BACK AT 1:00. The truth was that Sal had closed up so they could have a top-level powwow without the whole neighborhood listening. Sal would, of course, edit the material and tell the whole neighborhood later. Heaven had ordered pizza from their neighbors at D'Bronx deli and brought beers and sodas across the street from the cafe.

Sam was there, along with Joe, Chris and Murray. Sara was representing the kitchen. Sal and Mona Kirk sat in.

Heaven had just filled Sal, Mona and the front of the house in on the near miss of two nights before. Even the waiters who worked that night hadn't been told about the rhubarb tops.

"So then I told Bonnie Weber I thought the same person that killed Tasha surely must have planted the rhubarb, but I should have kept my mouth shut 'cause she, Bonnie, not Tasha, of course, pointed out how that wasn't necessarily the only option. Now she knows and she might have to close us down, for the public's protection." Heaven gulped for air. "So I guess we'll just have to solve this ourselves before they come and put a padlock on the door. Okay?"

"If you don't calm down we won't have to worry about being closed down 'cause you will have had a heart attack and we'll be closed anyway," Chris said.

Sam, being the youngest, saw this whole thing as a big adventure. "Sure, boss, sure. We'll solve it. What's the plan?"

Sal, being the oldest, saw trouble. "What did Detective Weber say about this 'do-it-yourself-find-the-murderer' shit? I bet she said butt out, huh, Heaven? I bet she don't want us sticking our nose in the police business. No, sir."

Sara had had the night and day to think. She was ready for action. "The police aren't going to lose their paycheck if this thing drags on, Sal. We are."

"Look, all I'm asking is for us to do a little research," Heaven said. "Think of why this might be happening, do a little footwork. Sal, keep your eyes and ears open. I don't expect you to act like Columbo, but people have been known to tell you their secrets. People get in that chair, and they just want to spill their guts. Mona, you too. I know you can talk on the phone and get more information in one afternoon than the whole police department could get in a week."

"What are we lookin' for, Heaven?" Sal asked.

"Anything that might be a clue to who wanted Cafe Heaven in trouble, or had the means to do in Tasha. Someone who has a big rose garden, someone who has a grudge, someone who knows a lot about poisons. If I knew what we were looking for, we'd be halfway there. Please, Mona, call your cat lovers. Shake the trees."

"What about the rest of us?" Joe Long had pulled a pad out of his backpack and was already assuming the role of cub reporter.

"I've made a list of all the possible motives I could come up with. I'm going to give everyone a motive or some investigative work. Then we'll do some research and report back to each other. Try to write down everything about your particular part of the picture. Even if it doesn't seem important to you it may make sense to someone else. Mona, Sal, same goes for you. Every time someone mentions Cafe Heaven or the murder, try to write it down. Even if it sounds totally irrelevant."

"Gotcha," Sal said. Mona nodded solemnly.

Heaven whipped out her list. "Here are the first things I thought of, work on them and if nothing comes of them, we can come up with more possible motives.

"First, of course is the distant hope that the real victim was Tasha and the rhubarb thing was just a smoke screen created by the killer who doesn't give a fig about us.

"Number two is that we could be a target for anti-gay groups. We do raise money for AIDS support groups and Chris has been in the news in the past. We also do performance art that deals with gay issues as well as other ticklish subjects. So someone could think we were all fags or fag lovers and want to get us for that.

"Third is the neighborhood. Could this be something to weaken the neighborhood or strengthen the neighborhood, according to your point of view? I know it's a rather paranoid idea but it could be real to some nut. It's the nineties, after all. People do weird things.

"Fourth, the disgruntled postal worker theory, you know, someone who was fired or quit and harbors a grudge.

"Fifth is someone who has it out for me personally. After all, I have been around Kansas City long enough to make a few enemies." She paused. "I could go on and on but let's stop with these possibilities. Now the assignments.

"Joe, I thought you could research the antigay groups. And I also thought we should try to find those creeps that beat Chris up. I guess they're out of the slammer, eh, Chris?"

"Are you kidding? Their sentences only lasted ninety days plus probation. Probation was over years ago. Do you really think I might be the root of all this trouble?" Chris asked. "I haven't received any new death threats, my mom hasn't gotten any presents lately."

Chris's mom had received dead gerbils a couple of times, wrapped in newspaper articles about Chris.

Heaven ruffled Chris's hair. "It's just one item on my list. God knows there are probably lots more potential suspects that I haven't even thought of."

Joe was writing furiously. "I'll go to the *Current News* office and see if they have a list of hate groups that might not like us, or me and Chris, at least."

Suddenly the whole room erupted with suggestions about potential troublemakers.

"What about that waiter you fired last month?"

"What about Angel Rodriquez? He's already been over to try to buy the corner."

"What about the leader of the Fudge Patrol, what's her name?"

"Remember that guy who came in every night at eight, said he had to see you, that he had been your boyfriend in 1969?"

Everyone was talking at once, raising their hands to get Heaven's attention like kids in second grade.

"Okay, okay, let's get back to my ideas," Heaven said. "Joe, you're going to do the hate groups, and I'll ask Bonnie to check out the guys that beat you up, Chris. Chris, will you take the Thirty-ninth Street League? After all, some of them were there Monday night. Maybe you could go visit Helen McDermott, see what vibes you get from her."

"Chris, I'll give you some history on the Fudge Patrol members I know," Mona piped in.

"Sara, will you go through the files to look up old employees who might want to start trouble? If any jump out at you as potential maybe you could try to track them down. I had completely forgotten that waiter who left last month."

Sara nodded a yes.

"Murray, do you think your old reporter skills are too rusty?" Heaven asked.

"Rusty, yes, but I'm not dead yet, babe. It's just like riding a bike. What's my assignment?"

"Well, Rodriquez is up to something, we all know that. But what? Maybe you could nose around at City Hall, look through the registry deeds, whatever. See if you can figure out why this old neighborhood is so hot right now. Maybe it's just gentrification but . . ."

"Got it, H. I'll poke around, see what's shakin'."

"What about me, boss?" Sam looked anxiously

around like the kid who hadn't been picked for Red
Rover, Red Rover.

"Sam, you've got to put down on paper absolutely
everything about Monday night. I know the cops
asked you a lot but I want you to try to remember
who was at every table. If you don't know them by
name then describe them, their clothes, their hair,
something. Try to write it like a story, you know, I
arrived at five-thirty P.M. and my first customers were
the blue hairs, that kind of thing. Then try to go over
every person, place and thing that came near Sandy's
table. Me, the busboy, the fudge ladies. Draw dia-
grams, give approximate times. No little piece of
trivia is too small. Don't take anything for granted.
You are the youngest of us and haven't had time to
lose your memory to drugs."

"It'll be an epic, boss."

"More like a cheap thriller, I'm afraid." Heaven
started throwing away beer cans and napkins, bringing back a semblance of order to Sal's.

"If they close the doors there won't be a thing
cheap about it." As usual Sal had the last word.

As everyone got up to go, Chris turned around at
the door.

"Wait a minute. Heaven, what's your assignment?"

"I think I'll tackle old husbands and boyfriends. See
if I can spot some bitterness turned bad."

"That'll keep you busy," everyone said more or less
at the same time.

Heaven knew she had two places to start, either
with Sandy or Jason. She hadn't told the crew about
Jason and Tasha. She just didn't have the strength to
answer all those questions.

Chapter 15

What woke Heaven up was one of Hank's hands sliding between her legs and the other hand gently insinuating itself into her mouth. Ah, the hands of a healing man.

It was Sunday and the restaurant was closed on Sundays. Thank God. Somehow Heaven and the rest of the crew had limped through the weekend business even though they felt the clock ticking. Heaven had been right about the sightseers. They had been packed both Friday and Saturday, a mixed blessing.

It was good because everyone suddenly felt like a squirrel who smells winter in the air. The waiters and bartenders didn't go out drinking with their tips this weekend, saying they thought they should put some money away, you know, just in case.

It was bad because no one had time to play junior detective. And the clock was still ticking.

But right now, for Heaven, time stood almost still for an hour or so. It was Sunday morning, Heaven and Hank could both stay in bed for a change. Lost in a universe of quilts and pillows and those healing hands, the ticking of the time bomb planted by Detective Bonnie Weber seemed an eternity away. It was almost eleven when Heaven and Hank finally stepped off into deep space, the floor.

"Why don't we just stay in the neighborhood today, H? Go down to Fifi's for lunch?"

Lots of Sundays, Hank and Heaven went to Southwest Boulevard for breakfast at one of the Mexican restaurants in that part of Kansas City. It was one of their only chances to eat out each week and they both loved food with heat in it.

"Do you think it'll be okay?" Heaven was hesitant to go to Vietnamese hangouts with Hank, and Fifi's was a popular cafe for neighborhood families, especially on Sunday.

"Of course it will. I told you, you just imagine stuff. My mother loves you."

"But she hates our romance, you know she does. Let's face it, honey, I'm not the kind of girl you take home to mother. I'm twenty some years older than you, and I'm a gringo."

"Heaven, don't start that again. Don't waste our time. Didn't you love what happened a little bit ago?"

"Of course. But . . ."

"No *buts*. Come get in the shower with me, and then we'll get dressed and go to Fifi's and have spring rolls and noodles and then we'll come back and read the paper. Come on, let me wash your hair."

Hank grabbed Heaven by the hair and slowly pulled her into the bathroom.

It was almost two before they got to Fifi's.

The church crowd had thinned out a little, but more than half the tables were still full, most of the faces

Vietnamese. During the week Fifi's was a favorite lunch spot for downtown office workers but on Sunday, it was mostly just the neighborhood. As Hank and Heaven sat down eyes turned their way.

"I told you this was a bad idea." Heaven was already blushing.

"Calm down. I'm starved." Hank spoke in dialect to Fifi's son who brought them Viet style coffee, a combination of sweetened condensed milk and espresso served over ice. Fifi waved from behind the counter. She and Heaven were friends through food. Heaven had asked her to be a guest chef at Cafe Heaven and had sponsored her membership in a new women's chef group. Soon their table was covered with crispy shrimp and sweet potato fritters, bowls of broth and noodles, condiments of lime wedges, bean sprouts, jalapeno slices, cilantro and mint leaves. Everything was going well when a group of Vietnamese teenage girls approached the table, laughing and whispering to each other.

"So, Hank, why don't you introduce us. Is this one of your teachers at school?" Hank's neighbor Su Le led the pack. She had loved Hank since she was in the third grade.

"No, Su, you know Heaven don't you? She lives around the corner in the old bakery."

Heaven could smell trouble, but she was trapped. She couldn't be a total bitch to these kids because that would be bad for Hank. But she knew *they* had no such qualms.

"Oh, yeah," Su Le said. "Aren't you Iris's mom? I guess that's how you two know each other, huh? How is Iris? Still in England?"

"Yes, Iris is just fine and still in England. At school. I didn't realize you knew my daughter."

"Oh, she was a lot older than me, but everyone knew her because you know, she had a famous father. Some old rock guy wasn't he?"

"Yeah, some ancient rock guy. Famous before you were born." Heaven was losing her grip.

"Are you coming home soon, Hank?" Su was playing to her crowd now, pleased with her own performance so far. "I need some tutoring with my calculus, and you're so good at math. Please help."

Heaven could almost feel the breeze of heavy black eyelashes being batted.

"Su . . ."

"Oh, he'll be home soon. I'll see to that." Heaven had lost her appetite.

The girls giggled and left.

Hank grabbed her arm across the table. "Don't do this, H. It means nothing."

"Let's get out of here." Heaven was throwing money down, trying not to look around at all the faces trying not to look at them.

"Okay, let's go home," Hank said hopefully.

"No, let's not." Heaven turned left as they hit the sunlight. "Let's go to the park."

Columbus Park, the neighborhood, actually did have a neighborhood playground and jogging trail. A park. Before crack cocaine, it was a place families would go on a summer evening to cool off and let the kids swing. Teenagers who worked around the corner at Jennie's Italian restaurant would neck in the park and drink beer after their shifts were over. Now no one went there after dark. Heaven and Hank went directly to the jungle gym. They climbed to the top and flung their legs over. Downtown Kansas City looked swell from there, like a real metropolis.

"Hank, you should just go to your mother's home and never come back to mine. You talked about me wasting time before, well, you and I both know that some day you're going to go off and marry someone your own age. You're going to be a famous doctor, have a wife and kids, the whole bit. So why waste any more time on this, when we both know what should happen." Heaven couldn't look at him. She studied her shoes carefully. Oh, great, she needed to shave her legs. This was just another reason Hank should never come back to her house, she thought. He probably would be glad not to have a girlfriend with hairy legs. Probably be relieved to be rid of her. Now she really felt miserable. And hairy. And old.

Hank didn't look at her either as he replied, but he did look hurt. "What should happen? What should happen is we go to the place I think of as *our* home and spend the rest of our one day off together. I traded around for months to get the same day off as you. We should love each other as much as we can. The future? Heaven, I learned when I was a little kid to not depend on the future. Yes, some day we might not be together. I might get smashed by a truck while crossing the street. You might have to be a grieving widow. Who knows who will leave the other first? There are no guarantees. I know that better than you."

"That's not the point. The point is I make you an object of ridicule in your own community. Those girls will tell their moms they saw Hank with his girl-friend. I can just hear them saying, Oh, Mom, she's as old as you!"

"This was my idea you remember. You didn't seduce me. I watched and waited, and the minute I saw that phony you were married to pack up I was at your door. Su isn't the only one in town who has had a crush. I wanted you for ten years. You were my teenage fantasy. When I grew up I went after what I wanted. Don't deny me my dreams."

"Then don't deny me a chance to feel sorry for myself for a while. God knows, I deserve it. A woman, who by the way was dining with an ex-husband of mine, died in my restaurant. Then someone slipped poisonous leaves into my salad greens. The police are threatening to close me down and a bunch of teenage girls were mean to me. Just go home, help that little witch with her homework, and let me have some time to pout."

"Heaven, let me help you. Don't shut me out."

"Don't be stupid. I just need to lick my wounds. I'll be fine."

The sun had gone behind some clouds and all of a sudden it was chilly up on the jungle gym. Hank and Heaven got down and walked to the corner in silence.

"I wish you'd let me come home with you." Hank turned to go in the opposite direction but he didn't cross the street.

"This is best. Trust me. I couldn't have made it through this week without you." Heaven felt her eyes filling up with tears. She had to move faster. She lunged for Hank's back and kissed him blindly on the shoulder, neck, arm. "That day you came knocking on my door was one of the best days in my life. Now go home."

"Just for tonight."

"Just for tonight."

As Heaven headed off to Fifth Street, Hank still paused. "Heaven."

"What now?"

"Call Iris."

Hank always knew what she needed.

Chapter 16

Angel Rodriquez had never learned to enjoy Sundays. There was a void in the morning where church used to be and an emptiness in the afternoon where Esther and the kids used to be.

The kids lived in San Jose now with Esther and her second husband. Angel saw them in the summer.

Most Sundays Angel walked down to the office and spent a few hours. Today he had puttered around the house, read the paper, made some eggs. Today he wanted no part of Rodriquez Enterprises. He was tired of thinking of business and tired of the fact he didn't have anything else to think about.

Monday was trash day in the Thirty-ninth Street neighborhood so Angel bagged his up, put his newspapers in a recycling bin and headed to the curb. It was late in the afternoon and the neighborhood was ripe with the smells of newly cut grass and charcoal briquettes lit for early Sunday suppers. He heard a racket from next door. It was Pearl Whittsit out with her sidewalk edger.

Pearl had a showplace garden and yard. Oh, not

one of those magazine gardens. No landscape architect designed it, and no lawn company came every
week and maintained it. It was all Pearl's doing, the
sweat of her brow and the work that had bent her
fragile body into a graceful curve. Pearl was seventy-
something, wiry and bright as a penny. She had been
Angel's neighbor all his life.

"Pearl, how's it going?" Angel yelled. She saw him
and turned off her tool.

"Well, well. Angel, how are you, boy? I haven't
seen you for a week or more."

"Fine, Pearl. Too busy. I don't get home until late
most nights. Busy time."

"I'd say you've been busy. A little too busy for me.
This neighborhood is changing faster than you can
say Jack Robinson. Why, your grandparents and my
George would never recognize Thirty-ninth Street."

"Except for Sal's."

"Oh, gracious, yes. It'll take more than you to run
Sal off."

"Now, Pearl."

"No hard feelings, boy. It's just difficult for an old
lady to change. Say, it's been a long time since I fed
you. What about it? An hour from now in my
kitchen? We can watch *Sixty Minutes* on that little TV.
I fried a chicken earlier."

"You've got a deal, Pearl."

When Angel opened Pearl's back door his head was
suddenly swimming with memories. His own kitchen
used to look a lot like this, before he'd remodeled it
for his new bride years ago. A painted wooden table
and chairs sat in the middle of the room. There were
old-fashioned cupboards with glass windows showing Pearl's dishes. Inside those cupboards, coffee cups

hung by hooks in neat rows. A window above the sink was designed for daydreaming while washing the dishes. No automatic dishwasher for Pearl. The gas range was a beautiful 1950s model with a grill in the middle. The refrigerator was a Frigidaire. Rag rugs placed in strategic places didn't completely hide the shining linoleum floor. A kitchen TV sat next to the coffeepot. The whole room was yellow and white enamel with houseplants everywhere. Pearl really had a green thumb. She was a good cook too.

Soon the table was full of things Pearl just happened to have around, the cold chicken, a Jell-O salad of course, some tiny new potatoes, boiled and drenched with butter. There were apples cooked into chunky sauce, fragrant with molasses. There was home-baked bread, put on the table on a cutting board so Angel could slice big hunks off. There was Pearl hustling around like a teenager.

"Angel, have I got a treat for you." Pearl sat down with a pitcher of lemonade in one hand and a plate of sliced tomatoes in the other. "The first tomato of the season."

"Pearl, it's only May. How'd you do this?"

"It's a new hybrid. I guess not all progress is bad. Eat it all, my stomach can't take the acid anymore."

"Why do you still grow them, Pearl?"

"For the neighborhood, boy. Everyone loves my tomatoes. And because I always have. Some things shouldn't change. Like my gingerbread upside-down cake which I just happened to make this morning. I know you love my gingerbread."

"You're right, Pearl. What would this street do without you, you and your gingerbread?"

Pearl's Gingerbread Upside-Down Cake

Melt 1 stick butter and 1 cup brown sugar together with 1T finely chopped ginger until the mixture bubbles. Pour into a greased 10" springform pan. Put canned pineapple rings and pecans on top of the sugar mixture. For a more modern version use pear quarters instead of the canned pineapple.

    2 cups all purpose flour
    1 1/2 teas. baking soda
    2 teas. cinnamon
    1 teas. ground ginger
    1 teas. ground cloves
    1/4 teas. cayenne
    1/2 teas. salt
    1 cup Crisco
    1 1/2 cups brown sugar
    1 cup molasses
    1/2 cup strong coffee, room temp.
    4 eggs, beaten lightly
    1 teas. vanilla

Combine dry ingredients. In a second bowl, beat together Crisco and sugar until light and fluffy. Add molasses, then coffee, then flour, eggs and vanilla until it is just combined. Bake gingerbread in the prepared pan in a preheated 350 degree oven about 1 hour, until a tester comes out clean. Cool 10 minutes or so and then invert on a platter. Unsnap the springform and gently work off the top (bottom) with a knife.

It was late now. Angel had returned to his house long before. He sat in the dark, sipping bourbon and staring out the window. As he watched, next door Pearl went through her house, turning off lights, closing windows. She checked the front door one last time before she turned out the porch light and headed for bed.

Angel was surprised to feel tears running down his cheeks. He remembered his grandfather doing those very same nightly rituals, those reassuring actions that you don't even notice when you're a kid. But somehow they make you feel safe. The neighborhood seems safe. And you don't realize that your feelings of security are connected to these small, inconsequential acts. Until there is no one there to check the locks anymore. Until it's your turn to make your family secure.

And what had he done to this haven of his childhood? Put in a strip joint down the street. Installed drug dealers in one of his houses in the next block. And it had worked too. Within six months he had picked up the houses on both sides of the drug dealer's house. For a song. From people a lot like Pearl and Angel's grandparents.

It's no wonder Esther left with the kids. He had taken the safeness away. Along with a lot of other things.

Chapter 17

It was after seven before Heaven got to talk to her daughter. She had tried as soon as she got back to the barbershop but Iris's answering machine had picked up.

Heaven had opened a bottle of wine, Ridge Zinfandel, and moped around for a while. Then she decided to go to the darkroom. She had been working on a book project for about two years now. Tonight was the perfect night to get something accomplished.

Heaven had been seeking out what she saw as the real backbone of American cooking, those black women with tiny storefront cafes, the good old boys who smoke ribs for a living, the restaurants where a whole Mexican family works together. She talked to them, asked for a recipe and then tried to photograph them with as much dignity as possible. She had some real gems, about seventy of the one hundred photos and stories and recipes she felt she needed for a good book.

She had a beaut of a Kentucky barbeque pit man.

She had a great one of her friend, Maxine, over on Thirty-first and Benton, working at the stove as usual.

She had two or three rolls of film on a woman making tortillas from scratch that she hadn't had time to print yet. Printing would be the perfect thing to get her mind off her troubles. It would also get her through dusk.

Even when she was little, Heaven had hated dusk on Sunday. It had always filled her with a sense of overpowering sadness and dread. She had loved school so it wasn't the fear of Monday syndrome. She felt her spirit leaving her at dusk on Sunday. If she went to the darkroom she wouldn't even know it was getting dark. She took her bottle of wine with her.

By the time Iris called she was a little drunk.

"Mom, what's goin' on? I just got up to go to the bathroom and found your message. It's the middle of the night here. You were cryptic."

"Drunk in the darkroom, honey."

"Tell me what's happened. God, now that I'm awake, you sound terrible."

So Heaven told Iris more or less everything and by the time she got done they were both laughing and crying with the absurdity of it all.

"Mom, I'll come right home if you need me. You shouldn't be alone. Where's Hank?" Iris knew Hank from the neighborhood and when she was home for Christmas she had learned about their romance. "How could he let you be alone tonight?"

"I made him go away. I wanted to be maudlin for a minute."

"It sounds like you've been very successful. How can I not worry? Are you going to get shit-faced down there and pass out from the chemical fumes? Should I call someone?"

"No, don't you dare. I can still navigate just fine, thank you. Don't you dare rat on me. I should never have told you I was tipsy. We have much bigger things to worry about right now. Enough about me. How's school?"

When Iris graduated from high school, her father had suggested she come to Oxford University and live with him a while. Dennis McGuinne had a beautiful town house in London, a country manor not far from Stratford-on-Avon as well as houses in Spain and the south of France. He was still a famous icon in the rock world and had also been producing documentary films on various painters and sculptors. The money he made for the songs he wrote twenty years ago still poured in. Or at least steadfastly trickled in.

Iris bopped around Europe like she had in Missouri and Kansas. She was at home in both worlds.

"School's just fine, Mom. I went to Ibiza with Dad last weekend. We had a ball. There's a new disco that no one goes to until five or six in the morning. They spray foam on you on the dance floor and no one has any clothes on."

"Iris! Don't tell me this! How's your writing?"

"I'm working on it, I'm working on it."

"Does that mean you haven't done a thing?"

"Mom, my tutor says I'm doing just fine. I'm worried about you. What if they close the cafe? I think I better come home."

"No way. You'll be home in six weeks or so anyway. And you must have to study for your finals or whatever they have there. Besides, we are going to find out who is doing this so don't worry."

"We don't have finals, Mom. Who is your 'we'?"

"Everybody at work, Murray, Sara, Chris. We all have our little assignments."

"Now I'm really worried. I know you love that sleuth bullshit. You always were trying to get me to read your old Nancy Drew mystery books."

"Iris, bye. I love you and I miss you."

"Mom, I love you too. Call me or I swear I'll tell Dad and he'll send me home on a private jet."

"Speaking of your dad, where was he last Monday?"

"Mom! That's crazy. Oh, sure, Dad just buzzed over to Kansas City to kill someone in your restaurant."

"I'm seeing a plot behind every ex-husband. I'll be fine when we find the real killer. Now hang up the phone."

"Bye, Mom. I love you."

Heaven was suddenly so tired. She finished rinsing her prints and put them on the drying rack. She rinsed off her trays and made notes about exposure times. She finished the wine. And sure enough, when she went back upstairs, night had come and it wasn't dusk anymore.

"Now all I have to do is get through the next week," Heaven muttered as she went up to bed.

Heaven's body was exhausted but her mind wouldn't shut off. Finally she got up and put her pink high-top tennis shoes on, along with the usual black tights and T-shirt. I might as well do something, she thought. Doing something meant revving up the van and heading toward Loose Park. Talking to Iris, and asking her where her dad had been Monday night had brought Heaven's thoughts back to the two ex-husbands she really did have to worry about.

Heaven headed south from Fifth Street to Fifty-fifth Street, the southern perimeter of Loose Park and home of Sandy Martin. Sandy owned a sprawling limestone creation of the early 1920's. It had sixteen rooms and a porch the size of a football field. Sandy's second wife, Mary, had chosen the house in 1970, when big, old houses weren't very popular in Kansas City. Because of this, they had gotten the monster for a bargain. Mary and Sandy had raised their two sons there and gradually replaced the leaky pipes and the noisy radiator heating. The rooms were full of antiques that Mary had collected over the years. The place was a real home, and worth three times what they paid for it in 1970. When Sandy became a partner in Klein and Klein, he could have moved to elite Mission Hills, over in Kansas, but Mary Martin had died of breast cancer in 1989, just as their youngest son went off to college. The kids and Sandy didn't want to move away from the house that had been Mary's kingdom.

Heaven had visited Sandy's many times over the years. She couldn't think of a time the visit had occurred after midnight. What did she think she would accomplish, banging on the door at this hour? Piss Sandy off, that's for sure. Heaven didn't even know what she wanted. Maybe she didn't need to knock on the door at all. She headed around the side of the house, going slow on the flagstone path in the dark. When Heaven caught the fragrance in the air, she realized what she was looking for. Roses, and she had found them. It must have been deep in her memory banks that Mary had a rose garden. Heaven saw the neat beds with dozens of bushes, spring varieties already blooming. Sandy obviously kept them tended. Did he do the tending himself or hire a lawn company? She was drawn down the garden path, but she stopped looking where she was going. The next thing she knew, no solid earth hit her shoe. She had walked in the goldfish pond. It was the noisiest splashdown in Loose Park history. There was the crash of broken glass. Heaven screamed and threw out enough water as she landed to land lock half the goldfish. The goldfish were all jumping and splashing and touching Heaven. She screamed again. Soon half the lights on Fifty-fifth Street were on and more than half the lights in Sandy Martin's house. Suddenly the backyard was ablaze with lights. Sandy was yelling, "I've called the police." His oldest son, Paul, appeared at the back door. "Hey, who's out there? You better split, man."

"Paul, Sandy, it's me, Heaven. Come help me out of this damn pond," Heaven yelled.

"Heaven, what in the hell are you doing here?" they said more or less at the same time. Paul trotted out the back door toward Heaven and the pond. Sandy marched the same direction, fuming.

"Paul, be careful if you have bare feet. I kicked something when my feet went out from under me and it broke. If you can just give me a hand getting out. The bottom is slippery." Heaven held out her hand.

Paul was laughing as he pulled Heaven out of the rock lined pond. "Haven't you been in enough trouble this week, Heaven?"

Sandy was not laughing as he stood with hands crossed across his stomach. "Very funny. What in the hell are you doing snooping around my backyard?"

Paul spotted the broken glass. There were three pieces that had formerly been a bottle. He picked them up carefully and turned them over in his hand. BLACK LEAF 40. Nicotine sulfate. Poison, the bottle label said.

Two patrolmen rounded the corner into the backyard.

Thirty minutes later, Heaven and Sandy were sitting on the front porch, rocking in wicker rockers. The police had been sent away, told it was a mistake. Sandy had refused to let Heaven come in the house to dry off, said she deserved to get sick, catch a cold. Heaven had started in on Sandy about the nicotine bottle. Paul had gone inside and rummaged up some towels for Heaven. He tossed them to her and said good night.

"You two, don't fight and wake the neighbors again, please," Paul said with a grin.

Heaven's clothes were very wet despite the towels she had wrapped around her. She longed to go home and get in the shower but she couldn't leave yet. She was going to try ignoring all questions about why she was skulking around in the dark. It's a good thing I did skulk, she thought. I found evidence. "Sandy, why didn't you say something the other day when I told you what the cause of death was?"

"What was I supposed to say? I had no idea there was nicotine sulfate around here. It didn't ring any bells. I don't keep track of every cleaning solution or bug killer either."

"Pretty damn amazing isn't it? You just happen to have the very stuff that killed your dinner date? I know Harry Stein would be amazed," Heaven snarled.

Sandy stared at Heaven coldly. "Not that it's any of your business . . ." he began.

Heaven jerked the towel tighter around her shoulders. She was chilly. "Wait a minute. You don't think it's my business? I'm a prime suspect and the cafe may be closed down? Give it a rest. I'm sorry I came over here so late and made a racket but don't give me that crap about it not being my business."

"Okay, just listen a minute, will you? When Mary died and both the kids were gone I seriously considered moving to an apartment on the Plaza. But the boys were hurt I'd even consider it. They didn't think it might be hard for me to stay here. They just wanted to be around the stuff that reminded them of their mom. I accepted that and when I did I started enjoying what Mary had given us. Maybe more than I had when she was alive." Sandy's eyes filled with tears.

Heaven felt terrible. She knew this was hard for Sandy but she could only think of the nicotine bottle. She had to ask again. "The rose garden?"

"Mary was so proud of her gardens. They had been on every garden tour and she had been featured in the *Kansas City Star*. I didn't know or have the time to devote so I hired the company that Mary used to mow the lawn and trim the trees. They also had a complete garden service. I guess that bottle didn't get put away last time they were here. Really, Heaven, if I were the killer, do you think I'm so dumb I would leave a bottle of the very same poison out in my backyard where it could be found so easily? Give me a little more credit," Sandy said.

"Sandy, I don't know what to think. There are so

many coincidences. You and Tasha. Jason and Tasha. You and roses. You and me," Heaven said.

"There is no you and me, Heaven. That's ancient history."

Heaven got up from her rocker and started unwrapping herself. "I still think of you as part of my life. Have you really erased me from yours?"

Sandy got up and walked over to Heaven. He took one of the towels and gave her hair a rub. With the towel around her neck he pulled her close to him. "Don't flatter yourself, Katy. I know where you're going with this. I did not kill to settle an ancient grudge because you left me in Topeka. Go home." Sandy kissed Heaven on her forehead. She kissed his nose and headed for the van.

"Why don't I feel reassured?" Heaven said out loud to herself in the rearview mirror.

Chapter 18

"Murray, have you turned to salt there, buddy? You haven't moved for twenty minutes. Have you had a stroke?"

Sal was powdering the neck of his latest customer and eying Murray who had planted himself in the chair by the window an hour ago.

"I'm watchin' the street, Sal. Watchin' the street." Murray lapsed right back into silence.

He had been up since dawn with a strange queasy feeling affecting his appetite and balance. He was starved and dizzy at the same time. After going to the Corner Restaurant on Westport Road for pancakes, sausage, potatoes, milk, juice, coffee and to read the paper, he realized what the feeling was. Murray was excited. He had been thinking about his assignment all day yesterday, and he had been making notes well into the night. It was the first time Murray had felt like this since Eva's death. It was like the old times in New York when he found himself right in the middle of a sticky investigation. He had to admit that he loved it.

Suddenly Murray saw Mona waving at him from across the street. She was out feeding her cats. Mona was like the Hindu temple keepers who feed the rats in India. Mona fed all the cats in the Thirty-ninth Street area. Cats who had perfectly good owners came to eat. Homeless alley cats came to eat. Unscrupulous folks who wanted to get rid of a cat were rumored to drop them on Thirty-ninth Street, knowing that they would be fed by Mona. This was feeding time so Mona and about thirty cats were communing. Murray waved back from the barbershop window.

"So, Sal. What's the biggest business on Thirty-ninth Street?"

Sal looked at Murray like he was touched. "What, are you nuts? The Medical Center, of course. Murray, you feelin' okay?"

"Just answer the question. No comments from the peanut gallery."

"And what state is the Med Center in?"

"Kansas, Murray. Four blocks from here in Kansas."

"And what state are we in, Sal?"

"Missouri, Murray. Still in Missouri as far as I know."

"Exactly my point!" Murray got up and ran out the door, leaving Sal and his customer shaking their heads.

"It's this deal with Heaven. It's got them all nuts." Sal started sweeping the hair clippings off the floor, chewing on his unlit cigar.

Murray had walked from the Corner Restaurant in Westport to Sal's. On Broadway he had headed north the block from Westport Road to Thirty-ninth Street and then hung a left and headed west. All along the way he made lists of the businesses on both sides of the street.

When he left Sal's, he kept going toward State Line and the Kansas University Medical Center. Murray had a couple of nurses to see. He loved nurses and had dated several in his life. This was the perfect time to visit, see what was shakin'.

One of the strange characteristics of Kansas City is that it straddles two states, Missouri and Kansas. The rest of the country doesn't understand this. They always introduced Kansas Citians as people from Kansas. The divided city also included several different counties in both states. This caused a slew of problems with police, taxes, city governments. The worst part was that most of the suburbs were in Kansas and the old core city was in Missouri. As more families moved to Overland Park or Leawood or Olathe, in Kansas, to escape crime and decay, the tax base of the core city, in Missouri, shrank. The crime, of course, eventually followed the bucks.

Thirty-ninth Street was a perfect example of this schizophrenic existence. It was like a lopsided teeter totter. Most of Thirty-ninth Street was on the Missouri side but the big, fat kid (the Med Center) was on the other side of the teeter-totter board in Kansas.

Murray arrived at the Med Center and slipped into the emergency room. He spent an hour in the ER waiting room chair, just watching the comings and the goings. Then he went to the cancer floor to see Lois Clarkson and the Lipid Clinic to visit Susan Waddell. It was after two when he stopped by the cafe on his way to pick up his car. He met Mona in front of her store where she was locking the door and putting a BE BACK IN FIFTEEN MINUTES sign on the door.

"I saw you coming down the street, thought I'd take a break and compare notes." Mona was clearly enjoying her role as junior G-woman. They went into Cafe Heaven together.

Sara was sitting in the office with employment files spread out all over the desk.

"Any luck?" they all said to each other more or less at the same time.

"Juan, the Cuban refugee who used to wear his pistol to work is at the county farm for a year. The kid with the long hair who walked out a year ago, high on speed saying he was going to blow up the block, is in Seattle. Or so his mother hopes. There are a couple of people that I would suspect of a post office type massacre but nothing that requires subtlety. But I still have a year to go. What about you?" Sara wanted good news.

Murray was dying to tell his whole theory about the Med Center, but he wanted to get to the Jackson County Courthouse first.

"I've got a list of every business and address between Broadway and State Line," he said. "I'm going to go check the ownership. Should take me the rest of the day. Do you need anything downtown?"

"Yeah, I have a couple of names I want to check out for arrests, but I think I'll call Bonnie Weber for that. It should be a lot easier for her than for you."

"I've got a friend in records, babe."

"I bet you do, Murray. But I'll call Bonnie anyway. Save your favor for when we need it. I also have a call in about the Nicaraguan freedom fighter that bussed tables last month. The one that just disappeared." She turned to Mona.

Mona frowned. "I have absolutely talked my ear off the last two days on that phone and I don't have one new good lead. Except I do know that Helen McDermott talked about Heaven at the last League of Decency meeting. Said something about Heaven's folks being good, God-fearing Kansas people who would roll over in their graves if they knew the kinds of things that went on at the restaurant. It was Helen's idea to picket at the cafe last week. How did Helen know anything about Heaven's folks?"

"And you said you didn't find out anything." Murray gave Mona a big kiss on the cheek.

She beamed. "I better go back next door. I have a new shipment of three-D water bowls with fish swimming in the bottom. Cutest thing you ever saw. Four of my regular customers are coming to pick them up today."

Murray turned toward the door. "Good luck, babe. Sara, see you tonight." He hurried across the street to Sal's. There was a wait of about three people. Sal was cleaning his clippers between two teenagers getting buzz cuts.

"Sal, I need a favor."

"Whadda surprise, Murray. Like?"

"When you get a doctor, nurse, orderly, anyone from the Med Center in here, pump 'em, okay?"

"For what, whose sleepin' with the brain surgeon? I can tell you that right now."

"Any news about expansion plans, mainly. Are they planning another wing, does their clinic have enough room, is the laundry overcrowded? Just get them talking, okay? Everybody loves to complain about their job."

"No problem. What would you guys do without me though? That's what I want to know." Sal said.

"Invent you, Sal," Murray said as he flew out the door.

Chapter 19

Joe Long was trying to look as cute as possible. He shook his dark, curly hair and sat up straight, head slightly to the left so his right side would hit the camera. Joe had always thought that was his best profile. And the camera, in this case, was the watchful gaze of Roger Dingman, editor of *Current News*, the Kansas City gay and lesbian newspaper. Joe knew with the cafe's future at stake he shouldn't be enjoying himself but there was no harm in laying the groundwork for the future, was there?

Joe had been born in Iowa, in a small town near the Missouri-Iowa border. His dad had farmed corn and soybeans, then the eighties arrived and the banks weren't quite as helpful to small farmers. Joe's dad couldn't make the bank payments and moved the family to the outskirts of Kansas City where he sold and repaired farm implements and riding lawn mowers. Joe started acting when he was three with organizing his Sunday school pagents. By the time he was in junior high, Joe was the director of an operetta plus the star of the Shakespeare festival that was held for all Kansas City students. When he graduated from high school, Joe's folks couldn't afford to send him to Missouri University. So Joe stayed at home and attended UMKC, the branch of the state educational system in Kansas City. It also happened to be the branch with the great theater program. Joe was the star of the department, graduated with high hopes to go to New York or Hollywood. But that took money. In the meantime, there was performance art at Cafe Heaven.

Joe had been single for about nine months now, an eternity in the eyes of someone twenty-four. His first great love, Carey Phillips, had moved to New York last year. Carey was also an actor and had been cast in an Off-Broadway play. Joe and Carey were still good friends but they had failed at long-term love. Carey had a new significant other and Joe didn't.

"So the main two groups against us are the reverend and the lady, right?" Joe had long, thick eyelashes and he batted them now.

"That's the most organized opposition. Of course, half the world probably was delighted when Chris was beat to a pulp. But the Reverend Cunningham actually celebrated it from the pulpit. I think I have a copy of the sermon he gave the next Sunday but it'll take some time to dig it out. That was years ago and we're not exactly computerized around here. The reverend sent it to us and we printed it. What gall, huh? On both parts. Know the enemy, that kind of thing."

"I wonder why he wasn't there Monday night, along with the Fudge Patrol and everyone else?"

"I don't think anyone noticed that you guys were fermenting revolution over there on Thirty-ninth. They thought it was just a cafe, maybe there was some music but now, Joe, the cat is out of the bag. I bet you have plenty of visitors for your Monday night soirees from now on. Are you having open mike tonight?''

"Of course. Heaven says we can't be intimidated. At least, not until the cops come and get us.''

"Is that a possibility?''

"Not unless bad poetry is illegal. No, they, the police, are a little afraid that last week may not be the end of it, that someone may try to cause trouble at Cafe Heaven again.''

"Has there been . . .''

"Nothing serious yet, but that's why I'm here. We're trying to help find the killer, or at least find the reason behind all the trouble. What about the other group, what's the name of it?''

"Well, I can see *you* aren't very socially aware.'' Roger was scolding Joe, but he was also flirting like mad. Joe bowed his head like a repentant schoolboy for a moment. Then he looked up like a kid with the answer to the teachers' question.

"She's from Blue Springs isn't she?''

"So you do know about her. Yes, the fastest growing suburb in Kansas City, Blue Springs, is the headquarters for B.U.R.N.E.D. OUT,'' Roger said. "The lady, the leader of the group, is Lena Simpson.''

"I was raised in Blue Springs so believe me I know the mentality. How do you think I could get my hands on their membership list?''

"For?''

"What if one of the assholes who beat up Chris is a member? Or a cousin or mother or sister of those creeps? Then we could give the police a lead, someone else who might want to cause trouble.''

"You sure make a cute private eye. Have you ever read Joseph Hansen?"

"Do you think the trench coat is too much?"

"No way. I'll make a couple of calls. I don't have their list because their main thrust is Planned Parenthood, the abortion clinics, the porn video stores. But B.U.R.N.E.D. OUT does its share of gay protest too." Roger got up from his desk and walked toward Joe.

"Are they the ones who picket the midtown churches, the churches that welcome gay members?" Joe asked.

"You got it. I guess you aren't as politically stupid as you let on."

Joe stood up. He smiled. "I don't give everything away on the first date. Do you think the Planned Parenthood office would have the B.U.R.N.E.D. OUT list?"

"Why don't I go over there with you. I know the executive director."

"I thought you'd never ask."

Chapter 20

Chris Snyder rang the doorbell again. He hoped she was home. This was his sixth house call and he felt ready to tackle Helen McDermott. The sound of a Chihuahua barking and running toward the door was hopeful. Sure enough, the Chihuahua had brought the mistress of the house with him to the door.

"Yes?" In speech as well as attire, Helen McDermott didn't reveal much. The chain lock, needless to say, was still on the door. Chris could see another cardigan sweater, another longish skirt.

"Hi, there. I'm Harvey Manson. I got your name from the Thirty-ninth Street neighborhood group. They said you were a leader in establishing the League of Decency and I need help. I live in the northeast area of Kansas City, and I am afraid that we should have started a group like yours long ago. Our neighborhood has become a cesspool, porn shops, male hustlers and crack cocaine everywhere. I wondered if you could just tell me a little about how to start organizing." Chris had dug out a pair of the most unattractive glasses he could find from his prop box and had them perched on his nose. He had greased back his longish blond hair and stuck a plastic pen protector in his shirt pocket. He hoped Helen was suitably impressed.

"Don't I know you?" Helen was staring through the crack in the door.

Of course, Chris wasn't going to give a shy smile and say yes, I was Barbara Bush the last time we saw each other.

"I volunteered last Thanksgiving at Grace and Holy Trinity. A wonderful job you do down there I must say."

"Well, thank you. We try." Helen was the administrative secretary at the Episcopal cathedral. The cathedral also housed a hot food program. They fed the homeless, two or three hundred a day. "I guess I could speak to you about our little group. If it will help the city I guess I have an obligation. But certainly not in a private place. After all, Mr. Manson," her voice rolled distastefully over the last name Chris had chosen, "I am a woman alone. I will meet you in fifteen minutes at the deli on the corner if you wish."

"I wish, Ms. McDermott, and I certainly appreciate you giving me your time. I would be honored to buy you a soft drink."

"Yes, well, this is not a social meeting, Mr. Manson, let's get that straight right now."

"No, of course not, of course not. In fifteen minutes then. I thank you again."

In two hours and fifteen minutes Chris was back in his own clothes and getting in the way in the kitchen at Cafe Heaven. He had his legal pad out and was reporting on his progress like a club secretary reading the minutes of the last meeting.

"Out of nineteen members total, I saw twelve to-day. Two of the couples, the Vladimeers and the Slowinskis live right next to each other. They're very religious, Catholics of course, and the men are retired. I got the impression that standing outside the strip joint and handing out fudge was just about the sexiest thing that had happened in any of their lives."

"Cheap thrills," Heaven muttered over the food processor roar. She was making artichoke hummus to go on a Middle Eastern plate they were featuring to-night.

Artichoke Hummus

> 2 cups cooked garbanzo beans
> 1 cup cooked artichoke hearts
> 6 cloves garlic
> juice of two lemons
> paprika, cumin, kosher salt, white pepper,
>   approx. $1/2$ teas. each
> olive oil

Combine all ingredients but the oil in the bowl of a food processor, turn on, and slowly drizzle in olive oil as the ingredients are being processed to a creamy consistency.

"Another couple live in that big stone house on Holly. Yuppies. All he could talk about was his prop-erty values, how if we didn't do something we'd all lose our equity, that crap. None of these couples took part in the Heaven march. They were all suitably shocked about the cross-dressing, the death, etcetera.

But another couple said they'd been to the restaurant and liked it."

"What about the members that were here? And how did you work Cafe Heaven into the conversation?" Sara was testing boiling pasta and chopping green onions as she spoke.

"That was easy. I just led in with something like, I saw your group on TV last week and that is what inspired me to seek your advice, blah, blah, blah. I don't have to say another thing for ten minutes. One woman knew everything that happened here last week and filled me in on the gory details. Her husband works at the Med Center at night as an engineer and is a frustrated cop type who also does shifts on the neighborhood crime patrol. Told me some hair-raising tales of purse snatching and armed holdups. I want him to come and walk me to my car from now on when I get off work."

"You tramp. He must have been cute. What about the others who *were* here? This is like the last episode of *Melrose Place* for the season, for God's sake." Heaven was getting impatient.

Chris continued. "Okay, okay. I'm coming to that part. Sylvia Schmidt is a computer records person at the Med Center. She bought her house three years ago and is nervous about her investment. She told me a gruesome story about her sister, who evidently was a stripper in Joplin fifteen years ago. It's a family vendetta against strip joints now. Sylvia is the mind slave of Helen McDermott. If Helen told her to jump off the Paseo Bridge, Sylvia probably would. She was certainly willing to come to Cafe Heaven last Monday, but her main interest is the strip joint."

"Did you see Helen?" Sara demanded.

"Helen and I had a lovely Dr. Pepper in a public place, thank you very much. I have the feeling that if Helen ever lets herself be alone with a man he'd be taken away in an ambulance."

"Chris! Is she a murderer or not?" Heaven was advancing on him with a colander full of blanched snow peas.

"Helen has possibilities. She knew all about your lurid past. But it was more like envy than hate. I think Bonnie should check to see if she's ever been in a mental hospital."

"Do you think she's nuts?" Heaven knew her voice sounded positively hopeful but she couldn't help it.

"Repressed, bitter, angry at everyone with a life, yes. Someone who would put nerve gas in the air ducts, no." Chris flopped the legal pad pages back into place, did a twirl and headed for the door. "I still have seven more League members to track down. I'm definitely going to have a performance piece when I get done."

"Let's just hope you have some place to perform. Has Joe showed up yet?" It was getting close to eight now, and the pace had quickened. Heaven could see this night was going to be busy with regulars and those who were hoping for a repeat of the excitement of last week.

"Heaven, I forgot to tell you something Mona came up with . . ." Sara began but was distracted by her pasta. It needed immediate draining.

"Reporting for duty, my fearless leader." Joe Long poked his head through the pass-through window.

"Don't come in here, we're too busy. But you've got to tell me what you found out today." Heaven left her station and moved over by the pass-through window and noticed food sitting there. "Sam! There are orders everywhere. Get this shit before it sets up on us. Oh, by the way, how's the show tonight, Joe?"

"Tonight is seventies retro night. We have lots of music, everything from Barry Manilow to Donna Summers' impressions. A little Carpenters sit-com, a little Bee Gees-on-tour skit, it should be wild. We have some angry seventies protest poetry too. People are still trying to sign up, but I think Chris has cut it off," Joe said.

"What did you find out about the hate groups?"

Joe's face lit up with pleasure. "Well, the big news is I have a date! Can you believe it? I went over to the *Current News* office and Roger Dingman, the editor, was so nice and helpful, and gorgeous by the way, and he went with me to the Planned Parenthood office and then he asked me to do something on my next night off which is tomorrow. Do I sound excited?"

Heaven smiled in spite of herself. "I'm not going to fall into the trap of asking why you two were going to the Planned Parenthood office. Birth control, perhaps? I'm very happy for you. I hope you'll fall in love and live happily ever after. Did you by any chance find out anything about the people who are trying to ruin our lives? And does anyone work here who can tell a brief, concise story?"

Joe continued at his own pace unfazed. "There are two main groups. The Reverend Emmanuel Cunningham who I'm sure you've seen on TV a thousand times. He's against everything. The last thing that got him on the tube was a book burning." Reverend Emmanuel Cunningham had led a group of irate citizens in a raid on the Kansas City public school libraries.

The libraries had incurred the reverend's wrath by putting books about gay and lesbian parents on their shelves. The reverend and his troops had stormed the schools, grabbed the offending tomes and built a bonfire with them in front of the Board of Education offices."

"Group number one," Heaven tried to keep Joe moving.

"Group number two is the lovely Lena Simpson and friends. B.U.R.N.E.D. OUT which stands for Brethren United in Revealing Naughty, Erotic Decadence. They 'out' the people involved in all the things they think are bad. That's why we went to the Planned Parenthood office, to get the B.U.R.N.E.D. OUT mailing list.

"They give Planned Parenthood a fit, picketing on abortion days and taking down license plate numbers which they then print with the name of the car owner. They must have a mole at Motor Vehicles. They 'out' the people who go to Planned Parenthood. Isn't that sick? They do publish a monthly newsletter which they send to those that contribute money to their war chest. The newsletter is where they out people—the owners of porno stores and video stores and sometimes the names of people who are HIV positive that they get from God knows where. They see these people as public health risks.

"Anyway, Roger and I got the mailing list for *Out News* from Planned Parenthood. I've already shown it to Chris and none of the names on it are the guys that beat him up."

"Sounds like a charming group," Heaven said. "Joe, you did good."

"One more thing. Roger thinks these groups really

didn't know about us before last week. He thinks we should expect—"

Before Joe could finish his warning, Sam made a beeline for the kitchen with Murray Steinblatz hot on his heels. "H, you won't believe what's happening out front. You won't like it either."

"A black guy in a minister outfit?" Heaven saw another long night ahead.

"And a bunch of white, polyester wearers with Dolly Parton hair, even the men." Murray was breathless from running the gauntlet to get in the door.

"And, and, the worst of all is . . ." Sam gulped before he could spit it out. "All four TV stations are here. Even Fox. A grand slam."

"Now all we need is the Fudge Patrol," muttered Heaven. On cue, the door from the dining room to the kitchen burst open and in marched Helen McDermot with Chris Snyder held firmly by the arm.

"Liar! You're a Liar! I followed you. I knew something was fishy about your story. You needed my help, my advice. Ha! Well, here's my advice to you, mister. Get out of this den of sin while you can! The wages of sin is death! You will all pay. And you, Heaven Lee, you lead these poor children down the garden path. You are the worst. You with your pony and your brand-new pickup truck and, and . . ." Helen was sputtering to a stop.

As usual, everyone else started talking at once. Sara started making soothing sounds, and gently removed Helen McDermott's hand from Chris Snyder. Chris made a run for the front of the house. Murray and Sam backed out the door quickly saying they would handle the problems in front. Joe came in the kitchen to help remove Helen. He took her out the back door, saying he wanted to repent. The only person not babbling was Heaven. Heaven was stunned. How did Helen McDermott know that as a teenager she had a pickup truck and as a child, a pony? All of a sudden, in that hot kitchen in May, Heaven was cold. She shivered.

"That's what I started to tell you before. That's what Mona found out," Sara said, "that Helen seems to know quite a bit about your life. Are you sure you don't know her?" Sara asked.

"Right now, Sara, I'm not sure of anything," Heaven said.

Chapter 21

Brian and Pauline and Heaven all trooped in the kitchen door. They had been out in the alley smoking. Brian, who didn't smoke cigarettes, and Heaven, who only smoked when she was at work, wouldn't miss these sessions for the world. The dishwashers, bartenders and of course the waiters could be found out there much too often. The smoking area was where all the really good gossip was passed in the restaurant business.

Heaven realized while she was passing on the news of last night, the pickets, the seventies' acts, the surprise attack from Helen McDermott, the progress Chris and Joe had made, that she had done nothing about her own assignment. She had put off everything, finding a lawyer, tracking down ex-husbands. She promised herself she would call the list of potential lawyers Sandy had recommended, but she wanted to give the team just a couple more days first. She could, however, review the husband situation while she worked, stuffing giant pasta shells with a ricotta cheese, basil and walnut filling. Now there would be time to think and the first person she thought of was not someone from her romantic past.

Since last night, Heaven had searched her memory for signs of Helen McDermott. Was she from Kansas? Did she go to school with Heaven? She certainly looked a lot older than Heaven but that was a style thing. Helen could be any age, from thirty to sixty. She did have a sensible Kansas look to her now that Heaven thought about it, a no-nonsense look that Heaven grew up with.

Katherine O'Malley had been a totally typical Kansas kid. Born and raised on a farm near Council Grove, Katy was ten when her dad put his farm acreage in the soil bank. The soil bank was an Eisenhower era invention to keep the country from losing all its topsoil and growing too much grain. It paid farmers not to grow crops. From then on her mom and dad had a ball, opening an antique business in the barn and traveling all around the midwest to attend auctions.

Katy even had her own specialty, antique jukeboxes which she bought and sold. Back then you could pick up jukeboxes for a song. She got a 1939 Wurlitzer out of a tavern in Strong City, a Seeburg Selectmatic 100 from the Sweet Shop in Concordia, a set of booth boxes in mint condition in Herington. Heaven still had the first 1949 Wurlitzer she ever bought. It was enshrined on Fifth Street in the bakery.

Katy was off at college and newly married to Sandy Martin on the weekend in 1966 when her parents were killed. They were driving home from a sale in Kahokia, Iowa, when a truck driver fell asleep and crossed the median. They died instantly, and Katy thought they must have been happy. They had gotten some good stuff at the auction from the looks of the wreckage. Katy took a broken doll with beautiful green glass eyes from the rubble. Her mother had been an antique doll expert. Even now, that broken doll stayed right by Heaven's bed on Fifth Street.

Katy's brother, Delmar, owned a feed lot in Alma, Kansas. He kept that business but took the family farm out of the soil bank as soon as he could. Del wanted to farm the land again. His wife continued the antique business in the barn.

Three or four times a year Heaven went out to Kansas for a family business meeting. She always tried to go when there was a good farm sale to attend. The memories of fishing through dusty cardboard boxes and searching through attics with her folks were still very dear.

The memory of those early years with Sandy Martin wasn't so bad either. Sandy and Katy had been married the summer after their first year at Kansas State University in Manhattan. Their's was a big wedding on Sandy's folks' ranch in the Flint Hills, complete with horse-drawn carriages and barbeque chicken and ribs and sausages and buffalo burgers from the Martin's own buffalo herd.

She and Sandy had been happy until they went to Topeka so Sandy could go to law school at Washburn University. Maybe if Katy had gone right to law school then too, maybe things would have turned out differently. But Katy was pregnant and had a stillbirth at eight months and then things were just never the same for them.

Katy felt alone. Her parents were dead, her baby was dead, her brother was busy reactivating the farm, Sandy was buried in law school. Looking back,

Heaven was sure she went a little crazy, probably there's a name for it, poststillbirth something. Whatever the name for it, the result was Katy went off to live in Kansas City in 1969, leaving Sandy to handle the divorce. He was mad at her until 1985 when they got drunk and slept together one last time. That had broken the spell and they had been friends ever since. Sandy was on Heaven's unofficial advisory board for life. Or maybe she'd been wrong all these years. Maybe Sandy hadn't forgiven her at all. She went over her midnight trip to Sandy's garden again. She hadn't mentioned it to anyone. She shuddered to think what conclusions Harry Stein would jump to if he heard about the nicotine. Heaven wanted to believe Sandy. Surely Sandy would have cleaned up his trail if he really did have something to hide. She reluctantly left thinking about Sandy with unresolved questions in her mind. She had to move on to husband number two.

The year 1969 was a wild time of drugs and rock 'n' roll for the nation. Katy was no exception. It was some time in this period that she worked at the strip joint, the Pink Garter, on a dare for a couple of weeks, found her name and her favorite hair color.

It was easy for a cute girl to get backstage passes in those days so Heaven also spent a lot of time backstage at rock concerts. That's how she found her second husband, Dennis McGuinne. Or how he found her.

Dennis and his band were in that first wave of English bands that conquered America in the midsixties. By the time they hit Kansas City's Municipal Auditorium in December of 1969, they were legends in their own time. Dennis and Heaven took one look at each

other after the concert and went directly to the hotel
together. The next morning they went to the airport,
flew to Nevada and got married at Lake Tahoe at the
glitziest wedding parlor they could find. They spent
New Year's Eve in Paris and January on the beach in
St. Bart's. In August when Heaven found out she was
pregnant, the party was over. Dennis was doing lots
of heroin, and Heaven knew that if she didn't leave,
she'd never make it to another New Year's Eve. A
baby girl was born on St. Patrick's Day and it was
Dennis's idea to name her Iris, after the famous English writer Iris Murdoch. Heaven loved *Under the
Net*, one of Murdoch's well-known novels, and so Iris
it was.

Dennis McGuinne sobered up fast in 1970 when his
best friend and drummer shot himself in the hotel
room next door to Dennis. The birth of Iris sobered
him too. Iris was his first child and she was a light at
the end of the tunnel of excess and tragedy. He sent
money, visited on every trip to America, and sent
tickets for Iris and Heaven to visit until Iris was old
enough to go to London by herself.

As hard as it was to have Iris so far away, Heaven
never hesitated when Dennis asked her to come to
England for university. Dennis had two children by
another marriage that was also over and Iris loved her
young half brothers. Looking at the situation now,
Heaven couldn't think of a reason in the world that
Dennis would plot against her and her restaurant. He
had a great wife, his fourth, he was still on the wagon
except for expensive French wine, and Iris and he had
just gone to Ibiza together. What more could he want?

As soon as she could after Iris was born, Heaven
started law school. She would have gone in 1967 if

she hadn't gotten pregnant. Now that she had Iris she needed to be able to make a living. Of course, Dennis would help but that wasn't the point. She couldn't depend on Dennis for every little thing. Heaven wanted to be able to take care of Iris and herself.

Heaven had always thought she would be a defense lawyer for the poor and downtrodden but her rock 'n' roll past came back to haunt her. When she graduated, a small firm recruited her to be their entertainment law specialist. Dennis threw her some good work, and of course, local bands that knew she was the ex-wife of Dennis McGuinne all hired her. She found herself busy and successful, and, in 1974, in love again.

Ian Wolff was a guest artist from Finland in the painting department at the Kansas City Art Institute. He had Leo Castelli for his dealer. He had a grant from the NEA. He had long blond hair and a killer smile. When Heaven and Ian met at an opening at the Kemper Gallery, the sparks flew all the way to Main Street. They were living together soon, married in a year. By that time, Ian wasn't teaching at the Art Institute anymore, he was lecturing at the Art Institute in Chicago, flying to Stockholm, selling to MOMA. They found a great warehouse down by the bakery for Ian to paint in. They flew to New York for openings and to Los Angeles for the Grammys. They were a multimedia cultural couple. Until 1982.

That was the year Heaven's world fell apart. It was the year Ian ran off with a Brazilian performance artist. It was also the year that Heaven got busted.

Maybe Heaven's mind was clouded with grief from the desertion of Ian. Maybe it was just the entertainment business in the seventies. She didn't exactly *sell* drugs. She just did what lawyers do. She put together a deal. Unfortunately one of the participants in the deal was wired for sound by the DEA. Heaven lost her right to practice law or be the President of the United States. She didn't lose her freedom though. A sentence of three years on probation sent Heaven scurrying for a new career.

Reviving her old interest in antiques, Heaven started dealing again, but this time it was jukeboxes, pinball machines, old slot machines. She also started cooking privately for parties. That's how she met Sol Steinberg.

Sol Steinberg was one of the few remaining members of what had once been a thriving garment business in Kansas City. His uniform company did not depend on trends for its success. It did depend on Whoopi Cola and Buster Burgers.

Sol's Unitrend Uniforms brought in a cool two hundred million a year, and a lot of it came from the two megachains.

Sol was a king among men. He was gentle and funny and most of all, honorable. Heaven liked him from the first moment she saw him. But that seemed to be how she always made her romantic decisions. Love at first sight. When he came into the kitchen at a party she was catering, complimented her food, said he was a widower and asked her to dinner she didn't hesitate a minute. It was 1985, three years after the heartbreak of Ian Wolff, the love of her life.

Sol Steinberg asked Heaven to marry him on her birthday in November 1985. She said yes. Heaven and Iris moved to Sol's big house in Mission Hills, the Beverly Hills of Kansas City. Sol was very understanding when Heaven didn't want to sell the bakery.

Keep it, Sol said, if it makes you feel better. It was a good thing she did.

When Sol died suddenly of a heart attack in 1987, Heaven and Iris were not in his will. They had been enjoying each other and their life so much. Sol gave her plenty of money, even stocks and bonds. Whatever she looked at twice he bought for her. And Sol was only fifty-five. It just seemed like they had all the time in the world. And when Sol had tried to bring it up, Heaven had hushed him. He knew he should go to the lawyer and take care of it, but he hadn't.

Sol's grown children gave Heaven plenty of time to move before they put the big old house on the market. They even gave her some shares in the uniform business. She had made their father very happy, they said. He had made her happy too. Heaven signed the stocks over to a trust for Iris.

It was time to hustle for a career again. This time catering seemed right. Sol and Heaven had entertained constantly. Their Sunday night soirees had been a hot ticket. Sol sent Heaven to Paris and Tuscany to cooking schools.

Now, back on Fifth Street, she had the room for a catering business. Room for baskets and pots and pans and a new industrial stove. Soon she needed a van to schlepp around in, and the jobs were slowly but surely trickling in.

One busy day in the spring of 1988 a designer called. He was working on a project for a restaurant in a warehouse, he said. He had heard she had done great things with her space, he said. Could he see it, he said. In six weeks he said, will you marry me? And Heaven Lee said yes to Jason Kelley.

He thought a restaurant was the next logical step.

So did she. Cafe Heaven opened in 1989. Jason gave up and moved out in 1992.

"Do you think you have enough of those shells done yet?" Pauline was watching Heaven for signs of consciousness.

Heaven looked down at the many rows of stuffed pasta and laughed. "I guess I thought I was feeding all those ex-husbands I was thinking about." Heaven lapsed back into her thoughts. Could Sandy have killed Tasha because he was in a mad rage at her for sleeping with Jason? Could Jason have killed Tasha because she was flirting with Sandy? No, this was planned out, thought out. Jason wouldn't just happen to have nicotine in his car and when he saw Tasha and Sandy together, decide to use it. It bothered her to think either one of them would hurt anyone. What if I'm naive and they both still really hate me. Sandy could hate me for leaving, Jason could hate me for opening this place. They could even be in cahoots, like in those Agatha Christie novels where the whole cast of dozens kills the bad guy together.

"Pauline, what if all the men in my life got together and hatched this complicated, diabolical scheme to make it look like I killed my customers?"

Pauline rolled her eyes. "Well, it can't be Sol. He's dead. And it can't be Hank," Pauline declared. "He adores you."

"Did I hear my name?" Hank strolled in through the back door.

"Hi." Heaven felt uneasy and shy.

"Hi. Didn't you listen to your messages last night? I called three times."

"I didn't get home until after one. We had another freak show last night. Of course, no one was hurt, thank God. But two different hate groups were marching and kneeling in prayer and—"

"I know. I saw the news in the doctors' lounge. Could I speak to you alone?"

Heaven walked out in the alley with Hank. She wanted to hug him. She lit a cigarette instead. Hank gently took it out of her hand and tossed it toward the Dumpster.

"Iris called me."

"That little rat. What did she say?"

"Take care of my momma."

Heaven reached out to Hank's open arms. "What a good idea."

Chapter 22

Bonnie was asking questions, to no one in particular. Sara was giving Bonnie a list of potential suspects that had worked at Cafe Heaven, folks that she was curious about but couldn't find with the address or phone number she had on file. Murray was waving copies of stuff from City Hall. Chris was passing out coffee and doughnuts. It was eight in the morning, an hour the dinner shift folks didn't usually enjoy. Today was no exception. They were at Sal's, of course.

Heaven called the meeting to order. "Calm down. Shut up. We only have Bonnie for an hour so let's get going. I'm going to call your name and you should give a report on your assignment. Bonnie, will you go last and tell us what you've come up with? I'll go first.

"Dennis and I have a child in common. He loves our child if not me. I can't see him hurting me in a way that would hurt Iris, by ruining my business and maybe seeing me in jail. I actually haven't talked to him this week but I just know . . .

"Ian Wolff broke my heart but why would he haunt me now? I should be haunting him, the dog. That and the fact I called his gallery in New York and they said he's still in Brazil rule him out.

"Sol Steinberg is dead.

"That leaves Sandy and Jason. Sandy had plenty of opportunity, I mean he was right beside the woman all night. I don't know if you all know that Jason was also dating the victim?" Everyone murmured under their breath. "I guess that doesn't let him off the hook. Both Sandy and Jason knew me and they knew Tasha and had relationships with us both. I guess you could make a case against either one of them if you really were pressed. And I guess we are really pressed but I still don't want to think that they want to hurt me or that they would hurt her." Heaven looked helplessly around.

"Let me worry about those two now." Bonnie Weber was writing on one of her legal pads. She had several sticking out of a big purse.

"Bonnie, you can. I've been worrying about them for years. Sam, you go next," Heaven said.

"Boss, I have a drawing of the room that night." Sam unrolled a beautiful diagram/drawing that indicated every table and who was sitting there. I have a copy for you, Detective." He handed a roll to Bonnie. "And here is my detailed account of everything that happened that night from when I scolded Tony to when Tasha collapsed. I also made a list of people I thought were weird, but I don't have a real suspect. I don't consider Jack a suspect. I know he threw himself on the victim but he thought it was an air raid of some sort. Really, Detective, he's cool in his own way. I included the couple at the bar." He paused. "You won't take any of this stuff and give it to vice or any other law enforcement agency will you?"

"Not unless it pertains to the murder and I can't avoid it," Bonnie replied.

"Well, the couple at the bar are, this is just a rumor of course"—Sam glanced at Heaven—"they sell cocaine. Then there was a guy who comes in most Monday nights and he always brings his guitar, or at least a guitar case. We haven't ever really seen him take out a guitar. We've joked about it before. Every Monday he comes in and we wondered if he was working up his nerve to play or if he was going to pull an automatic weapon out of the case. It used to be funny. Okay, moving on, I listed the Fudge Patrol because they were definitely suspicious. I also listed the doctor who dates all the nurses, but I know he was gone long before the trouble started. And, boss, I'm sorry, I put Sandy and Jason on the list too."

"I guess it just shows you're observant. Thank you, baby. Now, Sara," Heaven said.

Sara wasn't encouraging. "Most of the real nut cases that have worked at the cafe have been accounted for. I called Bonnie with a couple of names but she came up dry. They had no arrest records and they answered the phone at their present house and were working at a job. I'm still digging though, and I gave her three more names right now."

Heaven started pacing. "Okay. Thanks, partner. Joe?"

Joe had on his trench coat for the occasion. "We met our two hate groups on Monday night. The Reverend Cunningham and Lena and the B.U.R.N.E.D. OUT contingent. They were both there with bells on, but the thing is they didn't know anything about Cafe Heaven until the disaster last week. As far as we know, none of the thugs who beat up Chris are in either group. Our problems with the two groups are just beginning."

"Thanks, Joe. Bonnie, did you find out anything about Chris's attackers?" Heaven asked.

Bonnie shook her head. "Right. Two of the three are in Jefferson City, this time for armed robbery, which they badly bungled. The other one is in Salt Lake City at a seminary to be some sort of Morman lay priest or something."

Heaven was disappointed but not surprised. "Damn, that would have been so easy. Chris, what about the League of Decency?"

Chris brought a folded up piece of paper out of his shirt pocket. "Bonnie, can you find out if Helen Mc-Dermott has ever been in the, eh, a mental institution? I also have a list of all the Thirty-ninth Street League of Decency members. Could you just run them through the computer for the fun of it? Most of the folks I've already talked to are just in it to maintain their property values. That, or they are repressed religious zealots, or at the least, bored."

"Not very good possibilities," Heaven said, "but beggars can't be choosers. Murray?"

"Well, babe, I think I'm on to something but I've run into a hitch. Here's the thing. Rodriquez owns one hundred fifteen pieces of real estate between Broadway and State Line, on or near Thirty-ninth Street." The whole group came to attention with that announcement. "That is a hell of a lot of mortgages. I have three banks that seem to be the principal lenders that I have to check out, but most of these loans are backed by the Small Business Administration. I'll have to work more on that angle. So what is he, Angel baby, going to do with all these houses and storefronts? It makes sense that he would have some idea he could sell them to the biggest business around which also happens to be a growing business, the Medical Center, of course. So I think I'm on to something for all of an hour or two. Then I go down to the paper today and talk to my friend Jerry Lester on the business desk. He says that there's a state law that Kansas University Medical Center can't buy property in Missouri. No way.

"So if the Med Center can't spread over, then I'm shot down. Unless Sal has come up with a hot tip?"

"There are rumblings, Murray. I'm workin' on it." Sal was strangely quiet this morning.

"Mona?"

"The phone lines are practically melted down on Thirty-ninth Street. You heard about Helen yesterday so the only new thing I have is about Jumpin' Jack. He's the son of a very prominent Mission Hills fancy-schamcy family. Did we know that?" Mona had played her trump card with the finesse of a championship bridge player. "His father is Tom Gilbert of Gilbert buildings fame. You know, they manufacture those prefab buildings. The other two children, a boy and a girl, are executives in the family business. The Mrs. is a big society dame, lots of parties for charities. I guess Jack and the family don't have much to do with each other. They give him an allowance to keep him in shrinks and camo outfits, but they don't want him coming around and scaring the help."

Heaven shifted her eyes uncomfortably. "Actually, I did know that. I know Jack from before."

The whole room looked at Heaven, waiting for more. She was not biting.

"Bonnie?" Sal said expectantly.

Bonnie stuck her legal pad back in her big purse. "And you're all sure this guy is harmless? You guys are a piece of work. I need the whole homicide squad to keep up with checking out all your information. Thanks for all the time this must have taken. Chris, buddy, I promise I'll give Helen a look-see. I agree, it wouldn't hurt to check the other eighteen members out.

"Heaven, I'm checking the alibis of all your ex-husbands. This job may put the police department over budget for the entire year.

"As for me, I went through Tasha's life and apartment. I don't see anything there. Not yet. *Now.* Why don't we all go back to our chosen jobs? And as far as I know I'm the only one paid to solve crimes. I don't have time to tail you all so can I get a pledge of sobriety on this sleuth thing? Because, guys, we do have a murderer here, one that doesn't seem to want to be caught. You could be an irritating obstacle to the murderer if you keep poking around. Sometimes obstacles are removed involuntarily."

"Wait," Chris yelled. "One more thing." In one long rambling sentence he told how he'd been caught by Helen McDermott and about her surprise attack at the cafe. Bonnie turned to Heaven.

"What's the deal with the pony?"

"I did have a pony, and I did have a new pickup in high school. But I swear I don't remember Helen," Heaven said.

Bonnie pulled out one of her legal pads and made a note. "I think Helen is looking more and more interesting. Along with camo boy."

All of a sudden the door opened. A voice boomed. "Helen McDermott was across the street watching this building. She ran around the corner when I approached and asked her her business."

It was Jumpin' Jack, in full military camouflage regalia. "They let me out. Reporting for duty. I'm here to help."

Chapter 23

Angel Rodriquez saw his house. "Just a few more steps," he said to himself. "A half block at the most. You can do it." He staggered slightly. If his eyes would just focus. Then it wouldn't be so hard to walk.

Angel wobbled up to his porch but when he tried to lift his foot to go up the stairs to his front door, he just didn't have the strength. He sat down on the second of six steps. He loosened his collar. He felt so flushed, and, when he had seen his own reflection in the cleaners window, his face was bright red.

"I'd be sure I was having a heart attack, but I've felt like this too long. Since Monday morning when my eyes went out on me. If I was having a heart attack I'd be dead by now." Angel heard his voice as he mumbled out loud. He sounded like he was under water.

It was worse today, though. Monday and Tuesday he'd at least been able to work. Today it was only noon and he had barely been able to make it home. Should he just go to bed and sleep it off, or should he call for an ambulance?

Angel saw a cloud moving toward him. The cloud

was alive and buzzing, hundreds of tiny gnats swarming toward him down the street. Soon they were all around his head, tickling him, making him bat the air.

"Go away, bugs, you old bugs, you bugs you, you . . ." Angel was slurring his words badly. The cloud did go away, instantly, the bugs were not there. His eyes focused for the first time in two days.

All of a sudden the cloud of noise and wings returned and his dead grandmother was standing in front of him, snapping at the gnats with a kitchen towel.

"Get, now, get. Don't bother my baby." Yvonne Rodriquez shaded her eyes with her other hand. "Come on, baby," she held out her hand to Angel as she rose off the ground and started floating away.

"Gram! Come back. Get me, Gram." Angel forgot about the bugs and how his eyes weren't working and how he was too tired to take another step. He ran down the sidewalk, right into the arms of Pearl Whittsit. Pearl grabbed Angel by his arms and held on.

"Angel, boy, calm down now. You hear me, boy? Now I don't know what's the matter but you're coming with me. You look a fright. Come on now." Pearl led Angel around to the back door.

She had been transplanting some houseplants to their summer home in the yard, and there were empty pots and potting soil and a hand spade in the backyard. Angel somehow fell over a pot and rolled into the potting soil. He started batting at the air again.

"Now, son, get up. Let's go in the house and get some iced tea shall we? You look like you could use a drink."

"Yes, oh, yes. I'm so thirsty. I need water, water,

please." Angel staggered but made it to his feet. The promise of water seemed to propel him. Pearl quickly took a whisk broom from its peg on the back porch. She brushed the dirt off Angel. Soon they were in Pearl's kitchen. She had a water cooler of bottled water and she sat Angel right down on a chair next to it.

"Now, son, just drink as much as you want. I'm going to get a cold, wet cloth for your forehead. You look hot. We need to cool you down."

In twenty minutes, Angel had come back to himself a little.

"Pearl, I swear I saw Gram! But maybe it was just you. I haven't felt good for a couple of days."

"You're not feeling well, boy, so you want your Gram. You need someone to tend to you, that's all. I'm going to brew you some herbal tea that should fix you right up. I've got some chicken broth I made myself and I'll warm that up. I think I'll make us some nice sandwiches to go with that broth. How about a nice grilled cheese and tomato? Doesn't that sound good now? But first you need to rest and cool down. Come out here on the sunporch and stretch out on the daybed. I'll call you in a half hour or so. You rest now."

"Pearl, maybe I should go over to the Med Center. Maybe . . ."

"Oh, now, let's just wait until we have our lunch and you rest awhile. You already look much better."

Angel collapsed as soon as he sat down on the daybed. Pearl pulled the door to the roomy porch where she'd led Angel slightly shut. This was a former screened-in porch that Pearl had glassed in and turned into a TV room. It was full of houseplants and comfortable chairs. Magazines were neatly displayed in a big basket. She used a vintage iron and brass single bed as a daybed. Sometimes Pearl took a little rest there after she watched her "story," as she called *As the World Turns*. It was almost two when she gently shook Angel awake.

"Angel, you're moaning, son. Wake up now and have some lunch."

Angel couldn't tell Pearl that he had just seen Pearl's dead son, Gene, or that Gram had floated by again. He followed her to the kitchen and sat down. Soon they were eating soothing food, the kind of food you eat when you're little and have the flu. Pearl looked across the table with a stern expression.

"Now you know I never interfere. I've always respected your right to do what you think best. But I think you know I don't agree with all the changes you've made around here. I think you know I belong to the Thirty-ninth Street League. I felt I had to stand and be counted. And I know this sounds far-fetched but . . ." Pearl stopped talking and looked far away.

Angel grabbed Pearl's hand. The room was moving, and maybe if he held on to Pearl he could make the room be still.

Pearl came back from her reverie. "Well, I wonder if this sickness and this idea of seeing your grandmother, rest her soul, could just be your conscience trying to tell you something. You were always a good boy, Angel. You knew right from wrong."

"I still do, Pearl. I know you might not see it. But I still know."

"Well, son, you might feel a lot better if you just kicked those Spelling fellows out on their ear."

"It's too late, Pearl, too late. Could I have my tea

now? I'm so thirsty." Angel was twitching and sweating. His pupils were dilated.

"How is it too late? This is still a good street, full of good people. We have lots of families who love their homes, love this neighborhood. I know you're one of them, Angel. You'll never convince me any different."

"I'm sorry I've disappointed you, Pearl. I guess Gram is trying to tell me something, eh?"

"Could be, son. Could be. Now drink your tea. Those herbs are bitter, but I put the honey on the table. This will fix you up in no time. You drink that whole pot and then I'm going to walk you next door and see you to bed. You'll sweat it out tonight, you'll see."

Soon Pearl took Angel next door and helped him get in bed.

As Angel sank into sleep he saw his grandmother and grandfather at the end of his bed hovering in the air. Someone else was there too. It was Angel's dead father.

Chapter 24

Murray could hear his heart pounding. He could feel it pounding too.

It had been six-thirty in the morning when Sal had called, his voice squawking.

"Get over here by seven. I've got a lead. I already called Heaven."

Murray parked his Honda by the dry cleaners and jogged down the street to Sal's. He stuck his head in with a "What's shakin?"

Sal and Heaven were huddled around the coffeepot as though it were a campfire.

Sal poured Murray a cup. "A male nurse who comes in here every Wednesday sounds like someone you two need to talk to. He works the night shift, and I happen to know he goes to Bugg's bar every morning for a couple of drinks before he hits the sack. He should be there in another ten, fifteen minutes."

"Give us a hint, Sal," Murray said. "What's he up to?" Murray and Heaven were pacing like expectant grandparents in the OB-GYN ward.

Sal shifted into gear. "When I asked if there were

any new plans for more building over on Rainbow, he said there were big plans, but they were for this block, not Rainbow. And I said, couldn't be, this is Missouri. And he said there were ways around that. Then he said that he had seen some plans that would put a computer room right where we were standing. I laughed and said something about the hair clippings getting in the damn computers and he took off."

Murray was excited. "Plans, as in blueprints? Whoa, if there are already honest to God written down plans, we may be on to something!"

"Yes," Heaven said, "but how should we approach him? Could we see those secret plans to enlarge your workplace into another state, please?"

"Money, H, offer him an incentive," Sal said. "Sweeten the pot, kids. And remember he told me about it. How secret could it be?" Sal was staring across the street at the biker bar. "There he is, getting out of the Ford Bronco. Good luck, kids."

Heaven was already out Sal's door. "I'll be right back with the cash."

Murray spotted their prey, then shook Sal's hand. "Thanks for the tip. What's the guy's name?"

Sal grinned. "Lester, believe it or not, his name is Lester Grunfield. I didn't think mamas did that to their babies these days."

Soon Heaven came flying back across the street. "I found the three hundred we keep around to make change. I hope that's enough."

Murray pulled her out the door and trotted toward the biker bar. "Just let me do most of the talking, H, I've gotta plan."

"Fine, fine. I'm finally going to see you in action,

eh?'' Heaven could barely keep up with him. He was
like a hound after a fox.

When his eyes grew accustomed to the twilight
haze in the tavern, Murray saw Lester Grunfield sipping a beer in the first booth. A waitress was setting
down a platter filled with biscuits topped with white
gravy dotted with sausage bits. Beer and biscuits and
gravy. The strange habits of night workers.

"Lester, buddy. Murray Steinblatz. Heaven Lee.
Heaven owns the cafe down the street. Can we join
you for a minute?''

"I guess. Why?''

Heaven slipped in the booth beside Lester, trying to
look fetching even though she had neglected to comb
her hair or change out of the T-shirt she slept in.

"Lester, I used to work for the *New York Times*. Long
story short, I quit and moved to Kansas City.'' Murray slipped into the other side of the booth.

"Wow.'' Lester was digging into his breakfast. He
had barely glanced at Heaven. The waitress brought
another beer.

"But once in a while I still do a little work for them,
you know, when they have a story they want to check
out around here but they don't want to fly someone
in.''

"Hard times have hit everywhere I guess. Even the
New York Times is using stringers to save money. So
you freelance. Okay.'' Lester wanted the punch line.

"So I've been asked to check out a rumor that the
Med Center was expanding radically. They're doing a
piece on the new mega-medical complexes. I mentioned this to my old pal Sal. Sal said you knew more
than almost anyone, that you have your ear to the
door, so to speak.''

Heaven was counting out money as Murray spoke. When she had put five twenties on the table Murray stopped talking.

Now it was Lester's turn. "Well, I certainly don't eavesdrop if that's what you mean. This is going to come out soon anyway. I work in ICU. My big boss, the head of ICU, is on a long-range planning committee. Everyone knows we've expanded several blocks over on the Kansas side and that we can't legally buy property in Missouri. So the committee comes up with the recommendation that another company could be formed that would be able to hook on to the Med Center, provide services for them but not be a part of the university system and therefore not subject to the state bullshit. They came up with suggestions of how this could be structured."

"How?" Murray asked.

"Oh, I think I hear my bed calling. I'm just too tired to remember."

Heaven laid down another hundred. Lester picked it up.

The waitress brought a cup of coffee. Lester waited until she went back in the shadows.

"Tax-exempt cooperatives for one. Two or more tax-exempt public teaching hospitals, like K.U. and Saint Lukes, for example, can form these co-ops for the purpose of food service or a supply warehouse or clinical services. Or they could have their own printing press or a central billing place. Each hospital would pay for what they took: time, food, envelopes, whatever. The co-op can charge more than they pay for stuff just like a real business, and then at the end of the year they divie up the leftover bucks. Missouri couldn't touch 'em for taxes and Kansas couldn't nab them for building in Missouri 'cause it would be a separate deal, see. That's one of the options."

"Lester, I'm impressed. You sure know a lot about this for an ICU nurse."

"Well, Murray, some nights are slow. I read a lot. I put two and two together."

"What are the other options?"

"I'm getting sleepy again. What I'd like to do is maybe make a call for you to a friend of mine who knows a lot more than I do. If I could just remember her number."

Heaven counted out her last hundred.

Lester rolled his eyes at Heaven. "What are you, the bagman? I know you've had a hard week down the street but really, a bagman for the *New York Times*? Do you mind if I play through?"

Heaven wanted to make a smart comment about how any fool knows the *New York Times* doesn't pay for information like some "Hard Copy" show, but she had just invested three hundred dollars in this twerp, and she couldn't afford to make him mad yet. She got up so he could get up. Lester put the money in his windbreaker pocket and went directly to the pay phone. In five minutes he was back, tossing some of Heaven's money on the table to pay his tab and a card with a number over at Murray. "She'll be off work at three and thought she might like to stop at the Classic Cup in Westport for a cappuccino. You're buying. And my advice is to lose the bagman. I think my friend and you will hit it off better by yourselves. You'll see when you meet Earlene. She's the salt of the earth."

"My pleasure. I'll be there waiting from three on. Lester, it's been a pleasure doing business with you, right, Heaven?" Murray hoped Heaven wouldn't lose her sense of humor yet.

"It's been the highlight of the week," Heaven managed.

"Likewise," Lester said. "Give Sal my thanks. Tell him I'll see him on Wednesday, as usual. Oh, by the way, the cappuccino costs five hundred dollars this afternoon."

"Expensive coffee."

"The *Times* can afford it."

"Yeah, I guess they can." Murray just wasn't sure if Heaven could.

As they walked back, Heaven cringed at the idea of a shakedown. But she didn't think they had a choice.

Chapter 25

Murray got to the Classic Cup early, about two-thirty. He hugged Charlene, the genial owner, ordered a double espresso and studied his chart of Thirty-ninth Street that Sam had drawn for him. He also made one call to the *Kansas City Star*. It was nice to still have friends in the journalism business. The next thing he knew a spry sixty-year-old with a big blond hair-do was waving at him. Earlene Schumacher sat down with a thud.

"Oh, my God, what a day I've had. I'm Earlene Schumacher. Are you Murray? Or have I sat down with a total stranger? Of course, you're a total stranger too but you're *my* total stranger, right?"

"Murray Steinblatz, at your service, Ms. Schumacher. May I get you a cappuccino?"

"Mocha latte, please. And tell Scott to put lots of chocolate in it, okay?" Earlene, obviously a regular, waved at the counterman.

While Murray was at the counter he decided he'd better have another double espresso. He had a feeling he'd need it to keep up with Earlene.

Murray sat the foamy mug in front of Earlene, along with an envelope containing five one hundred dollar bills. She checked it and smiled.

"This is so exciting. The *New York Times*. When will it be in? You're not going to use my name are you? I don't think you should do that. I'd rather be one of those unnamed sources within the hospital, okay, Murray? But now, just call me Earlene."

"Well, Earlene, I'm not sure when this will be in. I'm just doing the research, the groundwork, as it were. And I can guarantee you I'll be able to keep your name out of the paper. I'll use my pull. But tell me, are you doing something you shouldn't? I don't want to get you in any trouble. Is there a problem?"

"Well, it wouldn't be worth five hundred smackers if you could just walk in there and find out about it, now would it? No, Murray, you're no fool, I can tell that already. But how many times in your life are you going to know something that the *New York Times* wants to know? Huh? Just answer me that, Murray?"

"You've got a point there, Earlene. Now tell me how this cooperative works. Is that what the plan is? Lester gave me the highlights, and I must say it sounds legal, slick and legal."

"No, no, Lester's a little behind. What we've got here is an ethical question, Murray. Probably legal also. Now let me go through this with you, honey. Pay attention."

"I promise."

"I work for a doctor, a big muckity-muck over there. Not the same one Lester works for. Lester and I both read lots of mystery novels. We decided to investigate. We pool our information. Keeps us young.

Both our doctors were appointed to this long-range planning committee. Big deal, see?"

"How many people on the committee?"

"Good question, Murray. Eighteen. Most of them are the heads of their departments. About half of them are doctors and half medical professionals. Medical professionals, for you civilians, are the people that run the billing departments, the operations, the food service. Along the way, everyone agreed it would be easier to start a separate company than get the Kansas Legislature to change the law that says you can't expand into Missouri. So now they have to figure out how to structure it, and that takes forever. Lawyers and doctors and architects would come and speak to the committee, they would fly off to see facilities other places. They finally decided."

"So, what's it going to be? Are they moving the kitchen and laundry?"

"Murray, you're a card. Now how could they make money off that? You silly. Okay, now stay with me. No, they decided on ASC and Subacute. Oh, for you civilians that's Ambulatory Surgery Center, surgery that you don't have to stay overnight for, and subacute is you know, when you don't really need to be in the hospital anymore but you can't go home yet, either. These departments are both the wave of the future, Murray, the wave of the future. Now let me give you the big picture and then we'll go back for the details. Somewhere along the way, some of the committee members started meeting on their own. Never in the hospital, but I'd have to go pick up lunch, and they'd go to the park. I knew something was fishy. The outdoors, for God's sake, for a bunch of doctors? Then, my boss asked me to type some stuff up. Type, for God's sake? Don't use the computer, he said. Well, it seems the committee members, at least part of them, saw dollar signs, plenty of them. They decided they should form the new company themselves, with of course, some phony front corporation. Lots of layers. And if all that wasn't enough they decided to stick a *huge* geriatric center over on the Missouri side too. Remember, the over-eighty-five-age group is the fastest growing age group in America, Murray."

"Do I look that bad, babe?"

"Oh, you teaser, you. So now we got a subacute, an ASC, a huge geriatric, but no, that's not enough. These boys put together a group to buy up the real estate that they would sell to themselves and their other partners. They hire Angel Rodriquez to do their dirty work, force down real estate prices so they get a deal. The small group that bought the real estate would sell the other bunch of crooks the land and make money. The bigger bunch would build the geriatric center which could tie into all the stuff the Med Center has that old people need. They make money again. Then there's the biggest group that owns the ASC and Subacute which is the only group that is authorized. And in the meantime these bozos are still making big bucks as department heads at a state-run facility. Now you and I both know that the folks who own the Med Center, I guess that's the taxpayers of Kansas, right, Murray, didn't mean for these greedy SOB's to make money off their prior knowledge, now did they? Why it's like Wall Street in the eighties, isn't it, Murray?"

"What about the blueprints or plans Lester mentioned?"

"One day a messenger delivered these, they're not

blueprints but drawings you get from the city, you know, plat drawings. Well, these had all the buildings that these yahoos have control of, all marked in colored pencils, green for one thing, yellow for another. It had every building between State Line and Southwest Trafficway down Thirty-ninth. And it dipped down on the side streets too. Now, Murray, I know what your next question is going to be. They're a little crumpled but here they are.'' Earlene pulled a wad of papers out of her enormous purse and waved them happily under Murray's nose. ''Before I gave the originals to my boss, I made these copies. We'll have to go to Kinko's together. I don't want to lose these.''

Murray practically knocked the chair over getting up.

''Earlene, would you like to have dinner with me? Maybe we could go down to Fedora's on the Plaza? Of course, after we go to Kinko's. I have so much to ask you. Will you marry me?''

''Not on your life, Murray. I hate cleaning up the bathroom after a man. But I'd sure belt down a martini with you and order the most expensive thing on the menu. Isn't this exciting?''

Chapter 26

Heaven couldn't wait another minute. This was the moment of truth. She bounded up the stairs of Angel's house and pounded on the front door with the energy of two Royal Canadian Mounties. Heaven was definitely going to get her man.

It was only seven-thirty in the morning, but she didn't want Angel to get away. Murray had called Heaven immediately after his dinner with Earlene. Heaven was determined to get Angel to admit he was the front man for the doctor's real estate scam. She wanted him to admit he was buying property at prices that people sure wouldn't sell them for if they knew what was really being planned. She wanted him to admit he put drug dealers in his houses and strip joints in his commercial space to drive down real estate values. Then, of course, she wanted him to admit he murdered a customer to run her out of business. Or had someone else murdered Tasha? It was hard for Heaven to see Angel as a killer but he must be a part of this evil plot. Or at least, Heaven desperately wanted it all to be tied up in a neat little tangled ball, the doctors, the strip joints, Angel, Tasha. She realized there was little or no chance of a full confession but maybe if she took him by surprise he would tip part of his hand. At least, he would know that someone had put two and two together.

Both Heaven and Murray thought it would be better for her to talk to Angel alone and away from his office. Angel would be less apt to suspect Heaven, he might take her for granted. After all, she had her own problems this week. When would she have had the time to investigate the complex schemes that Angel was involved in? Murray and Sal were around the corner at Sal's, they could be there in a minute if she called them. As Heaven knocked again, she heard some uneven shuffling noise coming near. Angel opened the door and Heaven forgot all her carefully rehearsed lines. Her mouth fell open in shock.

This man was in bad shape, face bright red, sweat pouring down his cheeks, pupils dilated to the size of big black saucers. He was in a pair of blue jeans and a sleeveless undershirt, like the ones grandfathers used to wear. This one was soaked in sweat. Angel staggered back from the door and almost fell over.

"I'm sick," Angel gasped. He reeled into the living room and collapsed in a chair. "Water, please, water."

Heaven found the kitchen and dug around until she found a glass, filled it with water and took it in the other room.

"Man, you must have had some night. You're a mess. Your eyes tell me you had a little coke, huh?" Heaven asked.

"No, Mama. No drugs. My dad come and my gram and Papa." Angel swatted at the air a couple of times. "Do you see them?"

"Your relatives?" Heaven glanced around.

"No, the gnats. How'd they get in here, Mama?" Angel seemed to be looking right through Heaven, as though she weren't there. He was batting at the air again.

Shit, this guy is having D.T.'s or something. I'd better say my piece, or should I call the paramedics? Or should I just leave? Heaven knew she wasn't going to do that. She was too wound up not to say her piece. She would watch Angel closely, be ready if things got any weirder, but no way was she leaving until she got a few answers. Heaven carefully sat down just out of the range of a quick punch or jab from Angel. For the first time, Angel tried to focus his eyes on Heaven. His head bobbed back and forth like a tether ball. "Listen, Angel, I'm sorry you're feeling bad but I'm feeling bad too. A woman died in my restaurant, next someone tried to poison everyone in the dining room, and I may be forced to close unless the police find out who's responsible for all this. I'm gonna get right to the point. I know that you work for a group who are buying up the neighborhood. I know they need Heaven's piece of thirty-ninth if they're going to finish this new medical complex. I think either you or maybe your partners wouldn't think twice about killing some customers to put us out of business."

Angel seemed to be listening, tracking with Heaven. He hadn't said a word but he had at least stopped batting at the air like a lunatic. Heaven plunged ahead.

"I don't have any evidence that you or anyone working for you killed Tasha.

"But I do have enough to go to Topeka to the state capital and blow the whistle on these guys. They used their position on the planning committee at the hospital for insider trading. I don't think the governor of Kansas will let them keep their cushy jobs when he hears what I know. Even without hard evidence I can put him on the right trail. He'll be able to find his way to the bad guys.

"The taxpayers of Kansas were definitely going to get the shaft from you and your partners. And so are all the people whose property values you've driven down and all the people you haven't paid a fair price to for their property already.

"I can stop this project. That's going to leave you with a lot of property and no buyer, Angel. Believe me, by the time I get through, you won't be able to sell a parking lot to a used car dealer.

"So what I thought you might want to do is come with me to see Detective Bonnie Weber downtown, and maybe you can give her some information that will help straighten this mess out. Because if it were the other way around and someone went to them and said let's make a deal, I think you know your friends would throw you to the dogs in a New York minute."

Heaven had rehearsed this speech carefully, but she hadn't counted on giving it to someone who could barely hold his head up. She had stopped trying to look Angel in the eye about halfway through, it was too disquieting. Now she turned back to see how he was responding and he wasn't, not to her, not at all.

"Too late. I think they . . ." Angel was looking over Heaven's head, like there was someone standing there. "They don't need me. They might have put something in my . . . poison."

"Exactly. Tasha was poisoned." Heaven was excited. It sounded like she was going to get something out of him after all. Then Angel fell on the floor, his body stiff, his eyes glazed. He was gasping for breath. "Shit," Heaven yelled as she headed for the phone. "He's trying to tell me *he's* been poisoned." Heaven called 911. Then she called Sal's and told the guys to hightail it around the corner. Angel was having trouble breathing, lots of trouble. All she could think of was a wet rag. Heaven went in the kitchen, found a dish towel, nice and clean in a neat drawer full of folded dish towels. That somehow reassured her. She ran water on the towel, wrung it out and took it back into the living room. She saw a shadow on the door window.

Heaven jerked open the door. "Murray. Thank God." But it wasn't Murray, it was Jumpin' Jack, slinking along the front of the house in his best SWAT team style.

"I have been performing surveillance. Are you all right?" Jack asked in his clipped, fake-military speech.

"I am. He isn't. Angel is . . . I think he's dying. Do you know how to . . ."

That was all the encouragement Jack needed. He was in the door and down on the floor re-creating the same techniques he had used so unsuccessfully on Tasha a few days before. As Heaven watched Jack do his version of mouth-to-mouth, she wondered if he could actually know what he was doing. Maybe what he was doing was what did them in, maybe Jack put some secret death poison from his mouth to theirs. Heaven shook her head and arms to shake out those disturbing thoughts. She had always considered Jack a tragic, harmless figure. Was she just becoming paranoid in the middle of all this madness?

Heaven went out on the porch just as Murray, Sal and the paramedics with their stretchers and oxygen came up the sidewalk.

An hour later, Heaven was sure of it. This day was never going to end. She just wanted to curl up in the fetal position, right here on Angel's porch. She was sure she would fall asleep instantly. She got up off the yellow metal glider and started pacing. Harry Stein looked out the screen door and sneered. Just my luck, Heaven thought, that Harry would be sent out here.

"Harry, how about cutting me loose? You've got my statement. I need to get to work," Heaven asked.

"Busy, busy, busy, aren't you, Heaven? But not too busy to come over here and send another one to the hospital. I'm glad I asked to be notified of all nine one one calls in this neighborhood, I wouldn't want to miss any of your numbers."

"At least he was still breathing. Look, I've told you the story. He was a mess when I got here."

"Right now, I've only got your word for that, Heaven. The paramedics think poison. What'd you do, bring Angel some of your cooking?" Harry ambled out on the porch.

"I know this looks bad but when you and Bonnie have a chance to check out this Med Center thing you'll see there are lots of people who might want to harm Angel. He might know too much, he—"

"Yeah, yeah, but why chase all over town for a suspect when we have a great one right here?" Harry sat down on the glider and looked up at Heaven. He looked like the cat who swallowed the canary. "Busy, busy, busy, aren't you, Heaven? But not too busy to make late-night house calls I hear."

Heaven knew by the look in his eye, Harry Stein

had found out about her visit to Sandy's. "Why, Detective, whatever do you mean?" she asked sarcastically.

"Did you take a little late-night snack over to your ex-husband's the other night? Or were you just there to take a little swim?"

Heaven could see she had a lot more explaining to do. It was nine A.M. This day really would go on forever.

Chapter 27

"**Y**ou've all got a lotta nerve, that's all I can say." Detective Bonnie Weber was perched at the bar between Heaven and Murray. They were all drinking champagne, the real stuff from France.

It was a combination wake and celebration.

The wake part was for Angel, who had expired the day before despite all the efforts of Jack and the Medivac team that answered Heaven's call. The paramedics said Jack did a good job.

The celebrating part was for Heaven and Murray and Lester and Earlene who cracked the greedy real estate scam that had almost ripped the neighborhood apart.

"I know none of you Junior G-Men want to hear this," Bonnie said, "but we don't have a clue yet who planted the rhubarb in the greens or who killed Tasha. Maybe it was Angel, maybe not. We don't even know the names of those involved in this whole hospital mess. And we don't know who killed Angel. But we do know what he died from."

Bonnie had stopped by to tell them about the lab results. She had been working late on another drive-by shooting over on Paseo. When Heaven saw her, she broke open the champagne and Bonnie hadn't had the heart to start her lecture. And for the first time since all this craziness on Thirty-ninth Street began, she had a glimmer of hope that it would all be cleared up. That seemed like a good reason to join in the celebration for a few minutes. But now she wanted to put the fear of God in them all. It was time for the amateurs to get out of the game, leave the cleaning up to professionals. She also needed to keep them all out of the sight of her partner. If he found Heaven at the scene of one more crime it would be all over.

"Well, tell, tell." Chris was jumping up and down behind Bonnie's stool. Everyone had gathered around. It was after midnight on Friday. No one was left but the help.

"The doc found lots of interesting things. First, cardiac glycosides, these two digitalis substances." Bonnie said.

Heaven put her glass down. "Digitalis? Isn't that what they give people for heart disease?"

"Well, these two"—Bonnie looked in a file folder that she had brought in with her—"convallarin and convallamarin, are not exactly the same as the usual digitalis given to heart patients. It is in the same family, just from a different plant. I didn't know that you could have too much of a good thing with heart medicine. It too can kill you in large doses. But as it happens, that's not all that killed Angel Rodriquez. That was just the tip of the iceberg, as a matter of fact.

There were also lots of nasty little alkaloids lurking around."

"Alkaloids?" Heaven felt the elation and relief of the last twenty-four hours fly away.

"Something complex, I gather from the doc. He said there are five thousand different ones. They all have to do with nitrogen, and they come from plants. This particular set of alkaloids"—Bonnie looked back at her notes—"datura stramonium, is used in asthma medicine."

Joe piped in excitedly. "Ah-ha! Asthma medicine and heart medicine. What a coincidence. A bunch of medical professionals are involved in an evil plot, and their minion is poisoned with medical stuff. Hello? Sargeant Weber?"

Bonnie closed the file. "No problem, Joe, that narrows it down to a mere two thousand Med Center employees. It isn't quite that easy. The alkaloid stuff is also the same stuff that's in belladonna, the hallucinogen. It's all in the nightshade family. It seems Angel experienced hallucinations, seeing his dead relatives, his neighbor reports. He also experienced extreme thirst, plus his pupils were dilated."

Heaven chimed in. "Yes, yes. He asked me for water and his eyes made me think he'd been doing cocaine."

Bonnie nodded. "The belladonna dilates your pupils for weeks, even if you just take the recreational dose. The doc said there are lots of records of victims batting the air, picking invisible things out of the air like you said Angel was doing, Heaven."

Chris was trying to piece this together. "Could we go back to Poison Number One? If it isn't the usual digitalis, what is it?"

"Well, the doc says most of the medical product is made from foxglove," Bonnie said.

"Wait. Aren't foxglove those tall flowers? That's heart medicine? I think I saw some of those somewhere in the neighborhood." Chris was trying to retrace his trail through the neighborhood on Fudge Patrol interviews.

Bonnie closed the file and tried to look stern. "They're very common, Chris. This is just why I didn't want you guys doing your own detecting. You start seeing intrigue in every yard. Now I'm afraid to tell you where the digitalis exotic that helped kill Angel really came from."

"Where?" Everyone yelled more or less at the same time.

"Lilies of the valley."

"Those cute little bell-like white flowers?" Heaven asked.

Bonnie nodded her head. "Right. The very ones. Doc thinks it, the lily extract, was in something that was already bitter and that Angel knew was bitter so he didn't notice. No one would drink it or eat it by accident because it tastes so bad."

"Who knew every cute plant had a secret life as an assassin?" Joe mused.

"But, Bonnie, how did Angel get flowers in his system? Doesn't it make more sense that someone dosed him with heart and asthma medicine?" Heaven was still clinging to the hope that this would all be wrapped up in a nice neat package.

"It makes a lot more sense. And they didn't find any half-digested flowers in his stomach, just a half-digested grilled cheese and tomato sandwich. The doc is doing lots more tests. He says he'll know more on

Monday. We're not releasing any of this until the rest of the tests are done. *Now*. Who knows what day it is?" Bonnie tried again to look stern.

"Friday," Heaven offered.

"Right. I want a pledge from everyone that no one will start interviewing the doctors at the Med Center or do any other half-cocked detecting, that no one will forget that we don't have a case against anyone for murder. Fraud, maybe. I have an appointment to go see the chancellor of the Med Center on Monday. A detective from the Kansas side is going with me. I also thought Murray should go, if he will." Bonnie looked over at Murray.

Murray nodded eagerly. Bonnie continued. "Until then, I don't want anyone doing anything. Understood?"

"How come Murray gets to go?" Joe was clearly miffed at being left out.

"Because I need him to explain this chain of events as told by Earlene. And I'm trying to not have to reveal Earlene as our source unless I really have to. I could be putting her in danger, after all. Murray has already put himself in danger. As much as I hate it, I'm glad you gave us this break. All of you. Now, kids, I'm outta here. No monkey business, no talking to anyone about it either." Bonnie stood up and drained her glass.

"So if the *Enquirer* calls we'll tell them we're holding out for the made-for-TV movie," Murray quipped as he headed for the front door. "See ya tomorrow."

Chris and Heaven headed to the back door after Heaven had locked up the front. She noticed a worried look on Chris's face and she tugged at his shirt-sleeve. "Hey, what's on your mind? I think we should try to relax now, let Bonnie do the rest."

"I'm just stuck on trying to remember where I saw foxglove. It seems fascinating now that we know it's a plant with a past."

"You know, Chris, I think I've seen those foxglove in the past couple of days myself. And I saw a yard with a big patch of lilies of the valley. I wonder . . ."

Chris gave Heaven a kiss good night as she climbed in her car. Heaven hugged him back and muttered. "I'll remember in my sleep. I always do." She quickly locked her doors as Chris disappeared in his old pickup truck.

Sometimes Heaven's van seemed to have a mind of its own. Tonight, instead of taking Heaven home, the van had gone south from Thirty-ninth Street to Fifty-fifth. Sandy Martin's house was in sight. The van seemed to park itself three houses down the block. Heaven would be more careful this time. She slipped down the street and around the other side of the house, avoiding the fish pond area entirely. It really was too dark for this sort of work, but sure enough, along the back fence, Heaven spotted tall blooming flowers. Of course, whether they were foxglove or not was another matter. Heaven didn't have a clue. Quietly, looking at where she was going, Heaven stepped in the flower bed and plucked one of the stalks. I'll just take this home and put it in water and go to the library tomorrow to identify it. As she made a beeline for the front and safety, Heaven spotted some small plants near the house. She grabbed a couple of them too. Stop while you're ahead, she said to herself. Sandy's house was completely quiet and dark. Heaven jumped back in the van and was soon headed downtown to the safety of Fifth Street. She knew it was silly but she was more afraid now than she had been since this mystery began. The end was near, she could feel it.

Chapter 28

Heaven turned south off Thirty-ninth Street on Genessee, and checked her post-it note for the address again. There it was, on the west side of the street. Nice bungalow, big front porch. Not one of the three-story giants that make up much of the neighborhood, but a nice house with a fresh coat of white paint. Even with fresh paint it somehow looked dreary. Those big, overhanging eaves always make a house look so foreboding.

Of course, Heaven knew she would see foreboding anyplace she looked this morning. Last night when she got to Fifth Street, she had fretted about Sandy and tried to call him with no results. Either he wasn't answering at two in the morning or he was out of town. Heaven suspected the latter. If Sandy had any sense, and he did, he would get out of town for the weekend, fly somewhere in his plane. Hank was at the hospital and Heaven had tossed and turned all night and when she finally gave up on sleep it was a little after six. She had gone to the restaurant and tried to concentrate on bookwork for a couple of hours. Now she was going to face the music and ask the question that had been haunting her for days, how did Helen McDermott know Heaven had a pony when she was a kid? After that she had to do some garden work. She had her plant samples with her, wrapped in a wet paper towel.

Heaven walked up the walk toward the house and found herself looking at all the neighboring yards. After all, Helen wouldn't have to grow those poison flowers herself. She could sneak over and steal someone else's lilies of the valley, for Christ's sake. Helen's own yard was quite pristine. Almost bare. Good grass. Some bushes that Heaven thought were spirea were planted in front of the porch. Or maybe they were lilacs. Heaven wasn't exactly a bush expert, having spent a considerable amount of time living in an old bakery with no yard. Of course when she had lived in Mission Hills with Sol Steinberg, they had a big yard, and a maintenance company to keep it up. Heaven suddenly remembered Jason and how he had always wanted a yard. Jason said he loved to garden. Did he know about foxglove and belladonna and lilies? Did Sandy? Helen McDermott appeared like an apparition right beside Heaven, causing her to jump and gasp.

"Helen, you scared me. Where did you come from?"

"I saw you coming up the sidewalk, then you just stopped and looked lost. I assumed you wanted to see me so I came out."

"I guess I did get lost in thought. I was thinking about flowers. Helen, do you have a garden?"

"Oh, certainly not. A big waste of time and money, if you ask me. Of course, I appreciate gardens. I just prefer to put my time in things that benefit the whole community. I can't see spending time on a garden when the neighborhood is being overrun with undesirable influences." Helen looked straight at Heaven.

Heaven decided to cut to the chase. After all, Chris had not fooled Helen. Any lame excuse Heaven might come up with, Helen would probably see right through. "Helen, why do you hate me? And how did you know about my pickup and my horse?"

Helen turned quickly and climbed the porch steps. She seemed more comfortable on higher ground. She turned and faced Heaven from this position with a little smile on her face. Heaven considered joining her on the porch but thought better of it. After all, she had a better escape route if she stayed on the ground level.

"You don't remember me at all do you, Katherine O'Malley?"

Heaven felt that chill again, the one that made the hairs on her arms stand up. "Did we know each other in school? Are you from around Council Grove?"

Helen nodded. "Alma, Kansas. Or that's where I lived when we went to grade school together. We moved to Kansas City when I was a junior in high school. But I sat two desks behind you in fifth grade. Do you remember that garden snake?"

Of course, Heaven remembered the snake. It had come slinking over her shoulder, and she had screamed. Not that she was terrified of snakes. Living on a farm she had been around plenty of snakes. But it had been so unexpected and she had screamed and thrown the small snake up in the air, and it had landed on Phyllis Langvardt and she had screamed and, well it had been like atomic reaction on a fifth grade scale. "Masie?" Heaven asked.

"Yes, Katy. I'm Masie."

Heaven couldn't believe her eyes or ears. But she did remember that Masie's name had been Helen May something. Masie had been like Pigpen in the Snoopy cartoon strip, the only kid always with a dirty face, clothes not ironed. Looking at the neat, trim, ironed blouse and skirt adorning Helen McDermott today, it was hard to imagine. Heaven remembered how all the kids had teased Masie. Her mother and father had separated when her father was stationed at Fort Riley, the army base near Junction City, Kansas. Masie's mother had moved to the small town of Alma and lived on a small military pension sent to the little girl. It was rumored Masie's mother drank in the daytime. No one else had a mother who drank. No one else had divorced parents. And no one came to school without having their clothes ironed. It was Eisenhower country, after all. "Masie, I mean Helen, did you put that snake on my shoulder?"

"You were so popular. You had birthday parties that I was never invited to. Everyone talked about your pony. I wanted you to get in trouble so I brought that snake and slipped it on the back of your desk when Dennis Athey went to the bathroom." Dennis sat between Heaven and Helen.

Heaven felt sick. If ever your sins come back to haunt you, you don't want it to be the sins of your unthinking childhood. How much it must have hurt that little girl to be left out. She was different from all of us, and we treated her like shit. Heaven wanted to take it all back but she kept thinking about Angel. Could what she did in the fifth grade have caused his death now? Surely not. Helen may want to get even with me but why would she kill Tasha or Angel? "I could say a million things to try to get you to understand, Helen. But really, there's no excuse. We were kids, and I'm sure we were brats. I'm sure I was a brat. I'm sorry I didn't invite you to my parties. I'm sorry you put that snake on my shoulder. Is that what you're doing again, trying to get even?"

"Oh, I've thought about it. When I see your picture in the paper it still makes my blood boil. But my opposition to those 'shows' on Mondays has nothing to do with you. And are you asking me if I killed that poor woman? Well, jealousy does not have to grow into madness. I realized when you were arrested and when your husband died that you didn't have such a happy storybook life. And your parents, of course. I am sorry about your parents."

"I was hoping that you would confess today, to something, Helen. And I guess you did. But this is not like Perry Mason. All the loose ends are still loose. Helen, do you want to try to . . . I mean would you like to have lunch and talk about our mutual childhood?"

"No, Heaven. I have no wish to relive those times. And I enjoy disliking you too much to give it up. Not yet." Helen turned. "You won't find the answers here, Heaven." She went inside and slammed the door.

Heaven was flooded with memories. The mention of her folks had set her back. She missed them for the first time in years. "Answers." Heaven muttered out loud. "I need some answers." She headed back to the van to go to the library.

Back in the neighborhood several hours later, Heaven saw the lilies of the valley first. They were planted on the north side of the house, in the shade.

She looked around at the smart hedges of yew, the carefully laid out flower beds. Her blood ran cold.

"Could I help you, young lady?"

Heaven whirled around and saw Pearl Whittsit standing there with a hoe in her hand. "Hi, I'm Heaven Lee. From the cafe. I'll love you forever for calling me young lady." Heaven waited for a response from Pearl, and when there was none she plunged ahead with her tale. "I live over in the West Plaza area, around Forty-fifth and Liberty. I bought a cute little bungalow over there during the winter so this is my first year with a garden. I want it to be really special. Of course I drive around and look at all the really fancy gardens over by Loose Park but I could never afford them. So I started looking for something more the size of my own yard, something I could manage myself. I think your garden is super."

"I'm surprised you have time for gardening, what with all the to-do up at your place," Pearl remarked dryly.

"It has truely been my salvation these past few weeks. I never realized what a relaxing hobby it could be. Gardening I mean." Heaven flashed her most ingratiating smile.

"Well, Heaven, there's nothing I like better than showing off my garden. Come along then."

Heaven walked and talked with Pearl Whittsit in a slow circle of the house. They passed the morning glories climbing up a wooden lattice, the hydrangea bushes, the bed where the daffodils had already bloomed.

"When you plan a new bed, Heaven, you want to stagger the blooming times of the plants, so that after the daffodils, something else will bloom up in that bed then something else after that. Most of my beds have something pretty in them until frost," Pearl explained.

Something pretty and deadly, Heaven thought. Sandy's small flowers were lilies of the valley all right but the tall flower had turned out to be hollyhock. Heaven thought hard about other gardens she had seen lately. She had remembered at the library, remembered that it was Pearl Whittsit's yard that she had been staring at two days ago when she had cooled her heels on Angel's porch, waiting to be questioned by Harry Stein.

Of course, she hadn't known who Pearl was, until she had called Chris this morning. They had compared notes and realized that they were thinking of the same house. A house Chris had tried to call on for his Fudge Patrol detecting. Pearl, who was a member of the 39th Street League of Decency. Pearl, who had been at Cafe Heaven on that fateful night. Pearl, who was the next-door neighbor of Angel Rodriquez. To her amazement, now everywhere she looked, she saw another poisonous plant.

"I need some tall flowers for the back row. What are those over there?"

Pearl pointed out the larkspur and foxglove and lupines. All poisonous according to the books Heaven had looked through. They discussed the English ivy and the Virginia creepers Pearl used to disguise the chain link fence. Poisonous also.

As they came to a huge rhododendron bush, Pearl laughed. "A funny story about rhododendron, these flowers attract bees but the honey is poisonous that comes from these blossoms. Don't want to plant too many rhododendron in one place."

"You're kidding! I didn't realize plants could be poisonous, but I guess that makes sense. Are any others poisonous? You better tell me so I don't kill someone accidentally." Heaven blushed at herself and the way she told such a bald-faced lie.

Pearl laughed. "Not much chance of that now is there? Lots of plants have some poisonous qualities. But those same qualities can be used for healing. Many of these plants were used by the Indians for medicine, in small doses, of course." Heaven was elated. It wasn't some horrible mistake. Pearl knew what she had here. And that remark about poison healing . . . Whoa.

Pearl pointed out the buttercups, the jack-in-the-pulpits, the pink caladium bordering a bed. The buttercups, she explained, were skin irritants. "In the old days, a fellow would make a poultice out of buttercups to make sores on his face. Then he would go out and beg for money, people would feel sorrier for him that way."

Pearl informed Heaven the jack-in-the-pulpits root is poison but could be cooked so that it was edible.

The caladium leaves contained needle sharp crystals of calcium oxalate that cut and burn the mouth. As they rounded the house to the north side again, Heaven paused in front of the lilies of the valley.

"Surely these aren't poison? I remember them from my childhood. I always liked them because they were so small."

"You'll like them for your garden because they grow in the shade. Not too many flowering plants grow well in the shade. But oh my yes, these are poison too. The story goes that even the water a bouquet of lilies were in, once killed a little girl when she drank it. Of course, these stories grow over the years. Come on in the house, Heaven, and I'll make us some lemonade."

Heaven stopped one last time on the way to the back door. "Oh, look, rhubarb. I love rhubarb. My grandfather always had a rhubarb patch. Is it hard to grow? And look at that huge tomato plant? How did it get so tall this early?"

"Well," said Pearl proudly, "that's a little experiment of mine. Both the tomato and the jimson weed are in the nightshade family so I grafted the tomato onto the jimson weed. It's a more hardy plant. It's bearing fruit too. This is the first year I've tried this, I guess you call it a hybrid. It should bear fruit longer than the normal tomato, until the frost. When we come back outside I'll cut you some rhubarb to take home. A rhubarb bush is a good thing to have around."

"Pearl, you amaze me." Heaven was amazed all right. Pearl must really think I'm a dummy to tell me all this. No way am I drinking her lemonade. Bonnie Weber's words of the night before were ringing in her ears, the words about the grilled cheese and tomato sandwich in Angel's stomach. She had seen the jimson weed at the library in the poisonous plants book. Heaven gloated. Wait till I tell Bonnie about the poisonous jimson weed and tomato science project. As they made their way into Pearl's tidy kitchen, Heaven spotted the water cooler.

"Oh, you know, Pearl, I think I'd rather have just plain water if you don't mind. I'm really thirsty."

"No problem, young lady. Now I have a favor to ask you. I usually would ask my neighbor, Angel Rodriquez, to do little chores for me. Bless his soul. I know I'm going to miss him. I wonder if they know how he died yet? The paper said something about convulsions."

"There wasn't anything new in the paper this morning," Heaven said. "I'm sorry you lost your neighbor."

"He was more than just a neighbor. He was my friend. I've known Angel since he was a little boy. I didn't agree with all the things he'd done in the neighborhood but you watch someone grow up, you develop an attachment." Pearl was silent for a minute, lost in her own world.

Heaven broke the spell. She wanted to get the chore done and get out of there. She knew just how much of an attachment Pearl had to Angel, enough to give him a poison tomato. She could hardly wait to get to a phone.

"What can I do to help you? You've been such a help to me with my new project." Heaven was certainly telling the truth there.

"I have a room down in the basement. It used to be my canning room when the kids were growing up, and I had a big vegetable garden. But now it's my potting shed. I keep all my pots and garden supplies in there and well, the lightbulb went out. The ceiling is just a little too high for me to reach the bulb on my step stool, and I hate to get up on a ladder. My balance isn't what it used to be."

Heaven breathed a sigh of relief. This would take no time at all. "Of course I'll change your bulb." She got up and Pearl quickly picked up the step stool that was out on the back porch. "Lead me to it," Heaven said.

When Pearl opened the door to the back room in

this incredibly neat basement, the smell of bleach overpowered them for a second. "Whoa, I smell Clorox," Heaven said as she adjusted the stool under the light fixture.

"Yes, I'm soaking some clay pots in a bleach solution. That way I kill any little bugs or parasites that might hurt my plants."

Heaven climbed the step stool and unscrewed the burned-out bulb. Pearl handed her a new one and took the old bulb out of her hands.

Pearl then moved with the swiftness of a youngster. She picked up a bottle of household ammonia and moved over to the ancient metal sink where clay pots were soaking in bleach. While Heaven was looking heavenward at the bulb, Pearl took a deep gasp of air, held her breath, poured the bottle of ammonia into the bleach and went quickly out the door, locking it with a slide lock from the outside. Toxic fumes filled the room.

The last thing that Heaven saw as she was floating into unconsciousness and onto the floor was a bottle of Black Leaf 40, nicotine sulfate, on Pearl's shelf.

Pearl went back up the stairs, threw away the lightbulb and put on the fire under the teakettle. She went out in the backyard and came back in with a handful of greenery. When her teakettle started whistling, Pearl poured boiling water over the leaves in a teapot. She had her stationery out on the table, powder blue sheets of Crane paper. Soon the herbal infusion looked the right color to Pearl, and she poured out a cupful and sat down to write and sip the brew. In a half hour or so, she went to the bedroom and got an old-fashioned lockbox down from the shelf in her closet. Pearl went back to the kitchen, poured the rest of the tea in her cup and threw the greens in the trash can under the sink. She rinsed out the teapot and set it in the dish drainer. Then Pearl sat down at the kitchen table again, with her tea and her lockbox. It was time to check the papers, the will and the insurance and all the rest. Pearl hadn't looked at her papers since Willis had died. Hadn't had a reason to. Until now. She drank down the rest of her tea.

Chapter 29

It was Saturday night at Cafe Heaven. Usually there was an early flurry of business made up of moviegoers who were trying to catch the seven o'clock show. Tonight wasn't an exception and the crew was all focused on work. So it was a surprise to everyone when Sara came to the window with a worried look on her face.

"Have you heard from Heaven?" she asked.

"No, isn't she in there?" Chris said, picking up a couple of Blue Heaven salads. "I didn't even notice. Don't tell Heaven that I can't tell if she comes to work or not." Chris thought back to his early morning conversation with Heaven. "Didn't she call?"

"No, she didn't, and she was the early man today. Since we're not open for lunch on Saturday, she should have been here by two. That makes her four hours late."

"Have you called her house?"

"Of course. I'm beginning to get worried."

As soon as they could, after the early rush was fed,

Sara and Murray had a conference by the bar. Jumpin' Jack was at his usual stool on the end.

"Murray, I think you should run down to Heaven's house. I know we need you, but Greg can hold down the fort." Greg was the second bartender on weekends and Monday night. "I tried to find Hank, I thought he could go over and check and make sure . . . but I called, and his mom said he had been at the hospital all day and probably would be there all night."

Murray looked scared. "What if she doesn't answer the door? Do I break it down?" Murray was skinny as a rail.

"Won't find her." A voice came out of nowhere with this pronouncement. Sara and Murray both turned toward Jumpin' Jack.

"Do you know where Heaven is?"

"Of course. I keep an eye out. I saw Heaven down on Bell. Went into the yard at twelve hundred hours, forty-six minutes. Went inside at thirteen hundred hours, twenty-six minutes." Jack checked his Vietnam issue watch as if those times were somehow imprinted there. "Did not come out."

"Jack, whose yard? And what do you mean she didn't come out?"

"I performed surveillance until eighteen hundred hours. Heaven had not emerged. I do not know the name of the individual but she lives directly next door to subject Rodriquez."

Murray felt a panic attack coming on. Why had Heaven gone to Angel's neighbor's house? "Jack, who lives there?"

"The unknown individual is a female in her seventies, I believe. She has an elaborate garden with very many flowers. Subject was showing Heaven Lee her flowers."

By this time a small crowd had gathered around Murray. Chris and Joe and Sam had crowded in to hear. The bar was also full of customers waiting for the second seating. Sara stared at the crowded room. "I have to go back to work and so do all of you. If we get behind now we'll never catch up."

"Wait," Chris said. He told them about the foxglove and how Heaven had called him this morning. "That house is where Jack saw her. I'll go find her."

Murray shook his head. "You can't. You have a station full of people. I'm the most expendable, and even though I wish we could just close up and all go, how hard can it be to get Heaven away from a little old lady, right?"

"An old lady who might be a poison expert and for all we know may have . . . Heaven." It was Joe who said out loud the words that they were all thinking privately.

"I better get shakin." Murray started for the front door.

"I will accompany you." It was Jumpin' Jack who made this offer.

Murray nodded his head. "I know I must be crazy but that sounds like a great idea to me right now. Come on, Jack buddy, let's check it out."

As Murray and Jumpin' Jack hightailed it down Bell Street, Jack insisted they stay near the bushes, in the shadows. When they got within a block of their destination, Jack whipped out a Slim Jim, the long metal device that auto clubs use to unlock locked cars, from the inside of his camouflage field jacket.

"What now, Jack? Do we steal a car?" Murray eyed the narrow metal bar with curiosity.

"You must proceed alone. I will circle behind. You will not see me. Do you know where you are going?"

"Yeah, yeah," Murray mumbled.

Jack headed down the side street in the direction of State Line.

All of a sudden, it was dark. It had been light just a minute ago, Murray thought as he walked, more slowly now, toward the house with the neat shrubs and trimmed bushes. As he reached the steps toward the porch, the most beautiful fragrance wafted his way. When his eyes adjusted to the dark, he saw Pearl Whittsit sitting on her porch swing, rocking in the dark.

"What is that wonderful smell?" That wasn't exactly how Murray had anticipated opening this conversation but he couldn't get over the sweet scent.

"Night blooming jessamine. Isn't it glorious? It grows better in Hawaii, but I coaxed it along. I wanted to be able to enjoy it when I sat out here of an evening. Just like tonight. Of course, those blossoms have a deadly poison, works just like strychnine. But that's the way with nature, now isn't it? The good and the bad are all a part of it."

Murray knew he was at the right place. "I don't know your name but I'm—"

"You're Murray Steinblatz, the famous journalist. I know who you are. And if I didn't know about you before, I know you were at Angel's when he died, bless his soul. I saw you over there with the police. I'm Pearl Whittsit, Murray."

"I'm concerned about the woman I work for,

Heaven Lee. She mentioned she might be coming over here today. Have you seen her?"

"Yes, and I must say she was much nicer than I thought she'd be after seeing her in that Godless place you work. She was so nice, I couldn't kill her."

Murray didn't speak. He didn't even think he was breathing.

Pearl got up from the porch swing. "Yes, Heaven was here earlier. I took her on a tour. She was quite interested. I bet you'd like to see my garden too, wouldn't you?"

"I don't know, Pearl. Isn't it a little dark for a garden tour?"

Pearl took Murray's arm with a surprisingly strong grip and propelled him down the steps. "Oh, nonsense, it may be my only chance to show you what I've done here. I've tried to make something that will last after I'm long gone."

Pearl guided Murray through the yard slowly and methodically, pointing out everything along the way and how it could hurt a human, the roots of one, the leaves of another.

Murray tried to remain calm when they passed near the cellar door that led directly from the backyard into the basement. He heard pounding coming from below. He also saw Jack working his way toward the cellar door. He needed to give Jack some time to find Heaven, who he suspected was doing that pounding. Murray stopped in front of the lilies of the valley.

"Are these what you used to kill Angel?" Murray could barely hear his own voice.

Pearl looked calmly at Murray. "Among other things. I didn't intend to create a garden of death, but creation and destruction are both right here, now aren't they? When I needed some ammunition for my battle, I found it in my garden." Pearl didn't seem to notice the creaking of hinges coming from the direction of the cellar door. Quietly, Heaven and Jumpin' Jack joined them. Heaven was leaning on Jack but didn't seem to be physically affected like Angel. Or Tasha. She grabbed Murray's hand. Pearl's expression didn't change. She looked far away.

"Can I ask you a question?" Heaven said. "Something very important to me? Why Tasha? How did you poison her? Why Cafe Heaven?"

Pearl looked at Heaven as if she had just noticed her. "I didn't know Tasha from a hole in the wall. It could have been anyone. It was my turn to make the fudge, so I fixed up a very special piece. The young lady just happened to be the one I handed the special piece to. I didn't know until I read the paper that I had been lucky enough to choose a person somehow connected to you. That night, while you were tied up with the police questioning, I went back in the alley to put the empty bottle in your Dumpster, but as I rounded the corner, I heard voices. I was afraid someone would see me by the trash, so I dropped the bottle in that little car. I knew it belonged to your husband, or whatever he is." Pearl paused and put her hand on her throat. She seemed to be having trouble breathing. "The rhubarb, I know you want to know about the rhubarb. I take my walk every morning, early, all around the neighborhood, and I shortcut up your alley sometimes on my way home from Roanoke Park. I've noticed the bags and boxes of vegetables. I knew they were there every Monday, Wednesday and Friday. I slipped some rhubarb leaves in with the other salad greens last Wednesday. The why? I think you know the why. You had to be closed down. We couldn't have you in the neighborhood. When I saw that poster, with men in women's clothes I knew that while we were down the street concentrating on the Diamond, on the naked women, the evil had spread. I couldn't let that happen. I had to stand and be counted. Now I've done my part."

"But we love this neighbor—" Heaven's plea was interrupted by a loud crash and a yelp from the backyard. It was Chris and Joe. Joe was carrying a hoe in a defensive position. They froze when they saw Pearl talking to Murray, Heaven and Jack.

Pearl glanced at them but turned back toward Heaven. "It's all right. I'm all done. I left a letter for that nice police lady, Detective Weber, is it? Yes, I explained why I had to do what I've . . . what I can . . . sorry about Angel, I really am. He had to be stopped. I don't know what got into that boy." Pearl crumpled on the ground like a used tissue.

"Chris, Joe, go in the house and call nine one one. Pearl, what did you take? Which one of these . . . ?" Heaven could hear Pearl's breathing becoming very labored, shallow.

"What's good enough for Socrates is good enough for me." Pearl's eyes fluttered closed.

"Hemlock, is that it, Pearl?" Heaven was frantic but she had a feeling that even knowing what Pearl had taken wasn't going to save her. So far Pearl's timing and doses had been perfect.

"She's a pro," Heaven muttered. Jack bent down and started mouth-to-mouth resuscitation.

Chapter 30

Heaven looked around her dining room table.

The bakery was a mess. There were empty champagne bottles, dirty plates, confetti everywhere. But Heaven didn't mind this mess a bit. She started humming as she loaded the dishwasher. It was Sunday, a week after the Saturday Pearl Whittsit had died. Everyone who had helped save Cafe Heaven had been around the table today, the staff, Sal, Earlene and Lester from the hospital and, of course, Detective Bonnie Weber and Jumpin' Jack. Mona Kirk came with Boots, the favorite of her cats. Heaven had insisted that both Sandy Martin and Jason Kelley show up too, even though it made Hank a little uncomfortable. Hank wasn't half as uncomfortable as those two. They were both having a hard time with their respective relationships with Tasha, and with Heaven knowing all about it. Time would solve that, Heaven knew. Time would also help the guilt Heaven felt for thinking Sandy or Jason might have been the killer.

Heaven had considered inviting Helen McDermott but she had decided against it. She was just going to have to accept the fact that Helen hated her. She would have to accept dislike from Harry Stein too, but she never even considered inviting him.

Heaven felt lucky to only be able to think of two people whose disdain she had to accept. She was a sinner, a felon, a person who had made more than one public mistake, and people did still like her. In a lot of ways her life had been blessed. If Helen was jealous after all these years, so be it.

Heaven had built a beautiful Torta Rustica filled with spinach and red peppers, cheese and ham. There had been a huge potato omelette, in the Spanish tradition, a platter of Italian sausages grilled outside on the Weber, and every breakfast bread known to man, bagels, muffins, donuts for Murray, lots of good Italian bread. They had toasted their good luck, had a moment of silence for Tasha and Angel and even Pearl.

Tortilla Espanola

    2 lbs. new potatoes, scrubbed
    2 sweet yellow onions
    extra virgin olive oil, the best you can afford
    4 cloves garlic, chopped
    6 eggs, beaten
    kosher salt and white pepper, to taste

Leaving the skins on, slice the new potatoes thinly. Peel, split and slice onions. In a large saute pan, heat olive oil. You need a good quarter inch in your pan. Saute potatoes and onions and garlic on a low flame until the potatoes are soft and the onions are translucent. Remove with a slotted spoon and place the potato mixture in a greased round cake pan, springform pan, cast iron skillet or terra-cotta baking dish. If you use something small, make two. Season eggs and pour over potatoes. Bake 20 minutes at 350 degrees and then start testing. When the middle is set and the top slightly brown, it's done. Let set 5 minutes, run a knife around the outside and invert onto a round platter. Serve at room temperature.

Murray and Bonnie had reported on their meeting with the Medical Center honchos. The Med Center bigwigs were horrified of the potential for bad publicity. They were in the business of saving lives not destroying homes and neighborhoods. They were going to proceed with an expansion plan that would take only commercial real estate, no family dwellings. The small businesses on Thirty-ninth Street that had been snatched up by Angel would be allowed to buy back their property at a fair price, then the Med Center would figure out how to best use the space they did have left. One building was doomed though. The big old theater that was now the Diamond was the first to be torn down for the future project. The Spelling brothers had already been given an eviction notice by the bank. The department heads who had tried to pull off this scheme were doomed too, doomed to be looking for new jobs.

Bonnie tried to explain all the poisons, the nicotine on the fudge, the spliced tomato plant, the lily tea. They all were amazed at Pearl's knowledge and especially amazed that ammonia and bleach create chlorine gas which causes unconsciousness.

Lester and Earlene gladly forgave Murray for the *New York Times* scam. This was still the most exciting thing that had happened in years, Earlene said. Heaven hadn't asked for the bucks back either. It had been money well spent as far as Heaven was concerned.

Everyone was gone now, even Hank who had been called in to sub for a sick doctor. Heaven was alone with the dirty dishes. As soon as the first load was sloshing away she headed for the basement and the darkroom. It was almost dusk on Sunday, after all.

It was six-thirty when Iris called.

"Mom, guess what?"

"What, honey?"

"I finally met her! It was so exciting. She was sitting by the front window of a tearoom right here in Oxford and I just went right in before I had a chance to lose my nerve and said, 'Hello, I'm Iris McGuinne and my mother and father named me after you,' and she couldn't have been nicer and the best thing is she's going to look at my writing! Isn't that super?"

Heaven knew, of course, that for three years Iris had been hoping to meet Iris Murdoch who taught at Queen's College. She had sat in on her lectures and had read every word Murdoch had published, but what Iris had wanted was something more personal.

"Oh, honey, I'm so excited for you. When will it be?"

They went on this way for a while, Iris telling her every detail of her meeting with Iris Murdoch, Heaven telling her about the party. Last week she had called Iris to tell her about Pearl.

When the call was over, Heaven rinsed her last prints. This week they were shots of a chocolate candy dipper at work. She washed off her equipment, turned off the lights. And sure enough, when she went back upstairs, night had fallen and it wasn't dusk anymore.

Now, all Heaven had to do was make it through the next week.

IF YOU ENJOYED THIS BOOK, HERE IS AN EXCERPT FROM LOU JANE TEMPLE'S NEXT MYSTERY,
REVENGE OF THE BARBEQUE QUEENS

Heaven jumped in her van that doubled as the restaurant catering van and took off. The cafe was located in midtown Kansas City, an area long on atmosphere and short on wealth. Most of the development in Kansas City was taking place south and west in Kansas, a situation that had cost the core of the city in Missouri sorely needed tax money. South and Kansas was where Heaven was heading now.

When she got to Fifty-seventh Street, just off swanky Ward Parkway, she hung a right and pulled into the driveway of a Tudor-style home. Heaven honked the horn and in a minute a tiny blond woman bounded out the door and hopped into the van. She was Stephanie Simpson, a food stylist for photography and film shoots. Stephanie was the Que—short for Barbeque—Queen in charge of making the team booth and food look great. Stephanie's husband was a lawyer which helped them afford the posh address.

"I'm glad you escaped. I was sure I'd get a phone call saying you couldn't leave your joint," Stephanie said.

"Tuesday is my best shot at getting loose. I can hardly wait to hear all the barbecue gossip. Did Alice and Barbara qualify?" Alice Aron and Barbara Jessup were two members of the Que Queens who also were on official competition barbecue teams. They had their own smokers and campers and everything.

Stephanie was filing her nails as they traveled. She was a fashion plate who received a lot of grief for being the only barbecue contestant with red nails. "Alice did and Barbara didn't. Thank God for us. We need one of them for their smoking rig and to boss the rest of us around. We can't let the boys whip our fannies again." The men had beat the women big time the last time they competed.

"Is Barbara pissed?" Heaven asked.

"She pouted all day yesterday, when the list of qualifiers was released, but I talked to her this morning and she was over it. She was planning a new dry rub that we're gonna mix up tonight. She thinks we should use it, but also sell it to make more money for the food bank. Did you bring all the stuff you were in charge of getting?" The members of the team paid for all the sauce supplies themselves so all the proceeds from sales could go to the food bank. A local radio station sponsored the competitions and paid for the meat both teams used.

"Sure did. Thai chili sauce and molasses and orange juice and bourbon, of course," Heaven replied. "Who's coming tonight?"

"Alice and Barb and you and me and Sally Jo and Meridith. You know, with our schedules it takes twelve to get six." There were actually thirteen members of the Que Queen team but because everyone had to make a living at something else, usually there were only six or seven involved in any one contest. Sally Jo Barton was the food editor of *S.N.O.B.*, a local magazine. Meridith Goodman owned her own catering business.

"Yes, and having more people makes for much better parties," Heaven said as she turned off I–35 and headed west on 110th Street.

The commissary they were heading for was located in a small industrial park in Lenexa, Kansas. The Kansas City Barbeque Guild rented the space and barbecue entrepreneurs shared it. It was equipped with large, free-standing stockpots, a bottling machine, and even empty generic bottles. You called up the Society, booked the space to rent, and brought your own food supplies and labels. It was a cost-effective way to comply with health regulations.

Stephanie looked up from her emery board. "So, tell me your news. How's the cafe? How's Hank? How's Iris?"

"The cafe limps along as usual. We have lots of customers but there still isn't enough money in the bank to pay all the various taxes and payroll and replace the seventeen chairs that are about to collapse with yuppies sitting on them." Heaven turned toward Stephanie and smiled coyly. "Hank is great. He only has one more year in residency and then I know it'll be over, but until then . . ." Hank was Heaven's boyfriend. "Iris was home for the summer, but now she's back in England, going to Oxford and living with her father." Iris was Heaven's daughter.

"And what does Iris think of Hank, pray tell?" Stephanie asked. Hank was only four years older than Iris.

"Iris knew all about us and met him at Christmas and she said, 'Be happy Mom.' I know he'll go off soon and marry someone his own age. I want him to have all that, a family, the stuff I've already done," Heaven said halfheartedly. She jerked the steering wheel of the van as they pulled into a parking space in front of a large, nondescript building.

"My, my, aren't you the generous one," Stephanie said smugly. She looked around as Heaven turned off the engine. "Could it be that we're early?" The parking lot was deserted except for a shiny new pickup with the words PIGPEN painted on the side.

Heaven looked at her watch and nodded. "This may be a first. It's only six-fifteen. We weren't due until six-thirty. Do you think we can get in? I'll unload the van to save valuable gossip time if we can," Heaven said.

Stephanie opened her door and jumped out. "The secretary at the society said someone else was using it today but they would be done by five. And since they are donating the space because it's for charity, I certainly didn't argue. But now that I see that awful Pigpen Hopkins' truck, I'm sorry I didn't ask who would be here before us. Do you suppose he's mixing up sauce to try and whip our butts again?" Pigpen was well known in barbecue competitions all over the nation. He also captained the team of men that competed against the Que Queens, the Male Chauvinist Pigs. He was known to cheat if the occasion and the prize money warranted it.

Heaven walked up to the door and tried to open it. It was locked, so she banged on it loudly. "Well, I'm sure Pigpen made it to the World Series so we won't have to worry about him lording it over us at our little competition at least."

Stephanie sniffed. "Oh, he'll find plenty of time to come around and give us grief. He's that kind of fella. His name fits him perfectly. Can you imagine being his wife?"

"Stop, don't take me there," Heaven said with her right hand held out, palm up, and her left hand over her eyes. She knocked loudly once more and yelled, "Oh, Mr. Pigpen, let us come in, let us come in."

"Not by the greasy hair of my chinny-chin-chin," Stephanie sang in a false bass. Pigpen had a beard. "I think there are delivery doors in the back of these places. Let's take a look."

Heaven and Stephanie started walking east, down the front of the building. The building housed various kinds of offices and light manufacturing. Next to the commissary was a computer software company and next to that, an organic potato chip distributor. Every three or four doors there was a walkway to the back. Heaven and Stephanie headed around through one of them and soon found themselves at the back door of their destination. There was a loading dock and a garage door, but it was closed.

"Pigpen, are you still there?" Heaven yelled. "Maybe he went with someone to have a beer and left his truck here." She tried the garage door and it went up an inch or so. Suddenly, out from under the door, came a thick, red substance, oozing slowly towards Stephanie's high heel.

"Yuk, what in the hell is that, H?" Stephanie reached down and gave the door a big tug. She was strong for her size. The door flew open this time and more red stuff ran out.

Heaven stepped to the side to avoid the red slime. "What an asshole. He must have known that we were coming next and trashed the place. He really is a pig."

The two women jumped over the goo and walked into the big kitchen. It was dark, but as their eyes became accustomed to the dimness, Heaven found the light switch and turned on the overheads. A sticky red trail led back to the biggest stockpot and it became very apparent what had caused the overflow. There were the stubby legs of Pigpen Hopkins, dangling out of the pot. His jeans were down from his waist showing those two inches of his bottom crack that he was famous for exhibiting. The rest of Pigpen was in the stockpot, headfirst in prize-winning barbecue sauce. He looked like he'd been there for a while.

REVENGE OF THE BARBEQUE QUEENS BY Lou Jane Temple—now available from St. Martin's/Minotaur Paperbacks!